REIGN

POPULATIONS CRUMBLE, BOOK 3

K. A. GANDY

THIGPEN-
GANDY
PUBLISHING

THIGPEN-GANDY PUBLISHING

To You,
For coming on this journey with me.

CONTENTS

ONE

ALLIGATOR SPIT

The gentle sweep of my thumb across the back of Patrick's hand is a constant, anchoring me in the moment. The steady droning of the aircraft has faded now, and my worldview has shrunk to here, now. I've lost track of how long we've been here in this dark room, surrounded by welded metal paneling—waiting, watching—hoping he wakes soon. Back, and forth. Back, and forth. After a small eternity, he emits a low groan, and the pendulum motion of my thumb freezes in the same heartbeat. Eyes riveted to his battered face, I'm still as a deer in the forest at dawn.

He winces, and on instinct I reach up and smooth back the dark hairs clinging to his clammy forehead. Stilling under my touch, he turns almost imperceptibly into my palm, and I release the breath I've been holding. It won't be much longer, now. The waiting is the worst.

Ever so slowly, his eyelids peel upward, but he quickly slams them shut again and winces. "Mhh—" he stops, clears his throat, the harsh sound breaking the pensive quiet. "My head is killing me," he says, in a shadow of a whisper.

"Patrick," I say, his name a benediction. "Thank the Lord you're okay." I force myself to be still, not to tackle him or hug him or any of the ten ways I'd like to get closer and jostle him, while keeping my grip on his hand calm, relaxed.

The corner of his mouth lifts in a wry smirk as he cracks his eyelids open again. "If you think I'm letting anyone or anything get between you and me, you're dead wrong." He slowly lifts his hand and brushes my cheek with his thumb. The tender stroke is my undoing, and the dam breaks, allowing my worry and fear to come pouring out of me in sudden, wracking sobs.

"Hey . . . hey—" His voice gives out again, but he wrestles himself up onto his elbows, and pulls my shoulders down towards him so I'm hugged against his solid chest. There in the shelter of his arms, I let it all out. After a few moments I begin to still to the firm stroking of his palm up and down my back. As the tears slow to a stop, I can finally hear his soothing, whispered words. "S'okay, Sadie, I'm here. You're not alone."

Wiping my salty tears away, I give him one final squeeze and then ease back so I can take him in. Frankly, he looks like death warmed over. "I'm so sorry, I didn't mean to break down. You've been out for so long; it was starting to feel like you were never going to wake up. And then you smiled at me, and I felt so relieved that I lost it . . ." I trail off as my wandering gaze lands on the plastic cup of water I'd brought in for him.

"Here, drink some of this! I know your throat must be sore." I snatch up the cup, nearly spilling it in my haste to give it to him.

With uncharacteristic slowness that belies his damaged state, he rests his hand on my forearm. "Sadie, it's okay. Give me a few minutes, half hour tops, and I'll be up on my feet. This isn't the first scrape I've been in. Thank you for the water, my throat feels like it's made of sandpaper." He finally takes the proffered cup, and drinks it down.

His eyes close for a moment in bliss as the cool liquid eases down his throat. "Much better, thank you. Now, the last thing I remember, we were all trying to get out of the bus. Clearly, we're no longer there, but I have no idea where we are. And what's that noise?" He looks around at the black-paneled room, the metal walls not giving anything away.

"Well, it's a long story," I say, not sure how to even explain all of the messed-up things that have transpired since the bus back from the beautiful little farm.

He gestures down his prone form, with a sarcastic tilt to his lips. "I think we've got a little time before I'm up and moving, and nobody's in here trying to rip out my fingernails, so I assume the kidnappers didn't get us. Lay it on me," he says, shifting positions in the bed so he's turned a smidge closer in my direction.

I run a hand over my braid, anxious without something better to occupy with my hands. "The bus wasn't that long ago. There was an explosion—you might remember that—that threw the bus sideways onto the shoulder of the road. So, the four of us were making a run for it, when an aircraft dropped a whole bunch of kidnappers right on top of us . . ." He stiffens, a hard glint returning to his eyes as the memory resurfaces.

"That's right, we were fighting, Peter had at least four guys on him, and I was almost to you when somebody grabbed me by the throat." His free hand reaches up and rubs absently at the bruised ring around his neck.

"Right," I confirm. "They jabbed you in the neck with some drug, which knocked you out."

3

His eyebrows shoot to the top of his forehead. "Wait, if they captured us. Where the heck are we? Is Peter here?" He scoots further up on the bed, scanning our surroundings with a much more critical eye. He starts to swing his legs over, but I reach up and stop him.

"Patrick, please stay in bed for a little while longer. You had quite an ordeal, and we don't know how long it will take for the drugs to be fully out of your system. Plus, I don't think it will be much longer before we get there, and then you'll have to be up and moving. And no, Peter isn't here." Worry drags at my conscience, and I hate that we don't have any information about what state he was left in. *He can't be dead. Please, don't let him be dead!*

He acquiesces and leans back against the cold wall with a grimace, his thin t-shirt not doing much to protect him from the chill. He doesn't relax, but remains on high alert despite his injuries.

"Anyways, I don't know where we are exactly. We're still in the air, and I have no idea how long we've been in the air. I woke up next to you a little while ago, but we were already flying." I take a deep breath, bolstering myself for the next bit. "Atlas and Nell are here, too. I snuck down the hall trying to find out who had us, and found them in a meeting room with our captors. Apparently . . . there's a resistance group, and that's who snatched us."

His deep, denim-blue eyes turned icy in an instant. "What do you mean, a resistance group? *The* Resistance, or someone else? And how are Nell and Atlas here? Wait, did Atlas—was he in on this?" His spine stiffens, and he lurches forward on the bed, anger simmering.

Raising both hands in a calming gesture, I try to console him, "I don't really know yet. Atlas admitted to knowing them, but I don't know how far it goes. If he's part of the uprising, or if they're

4

just the tool he used to get us away from the resort . . . but I have to say, my gut says we should be wary. Especially if he didn't tell you, either." The last sentence leaves my mouth barely above a whisper, as I gauge his reaction carefully. I hate to think that Patrick would have kept another major secret from me, but, I have to acknowledge that it's possible he knew about Atlas's plan.

His lips press together in an angry line, and his eyebrows drop. "Sadie, do you really think I would keep something like this from you? I learned my lesson the first time. What I know, you know. And Atlas is going to have some serious explaining to do, because no *way* am I okay with cozying up to some far-out nut job Resistance against my father. No way." Once again, he tries to rise from the bed. I have both hands on his shoulders, trying to reason with him when the tempo of the aircraft's engines changes, and my stomach flies up into my throat. The sudden plunging sensation causes me to lurch forward and land on top of Patrick in a heap.

I try to right myself after a few seconds of detangling our limbs, but our sudden, sharp descent halts abruptly before I can make it back to my seat, once again dumping me atop him. The jarring landing is followed by deafening silence as the engines are cut. Sitting back in the chair, I rub my ear. The sound of the flight had been so constant—like a bumblebee directly out of sight—that my ears feel strange now that it's finally stopped.

Patrick lurches to his feet, taking advantage of my distraction, and quickly scans the room. "I'm guessing they didn't leave my pistol, did they?" he asks wryly.

"Uh, well, I didn't think to check," I admit sheepishly. "I was so focused on you and where we were, that I didn't even look for our things." I stand and rifle through a few of the cabinets lining the far wall, and find a heap of our belongings at the bottom. Sifting through them, I see fresh clothes and a few small personal items, but no weapons of any kind. Before I can report my findings, the door swings open with a sigh, and I spin on my heel to find Patrick between me and the door, already in a defensive stance.

His adrenalin must have burned off the last of the sedatives because he is steady as a rock in front of me. Nell strides into the room a moment later, only to stop and slowly raise her palms.

"Hey, Patrick, it's just me. Are you okay? I was worried about you," she says in her usual rambling-yet-rushed way.

Patrick's tension visibly drains away, and he sways on his feet. I step up to his side and thread his arm over my shoulders for support.

"Well, uh, we're here." Nell says, pointing over her shoulder with her thumb.

"Where's here?" Patrick says in a no-nonsense tone.

"They didn't tell me, but I think we're somewhere in Missiana. From the glimpse I caught of the landscape, it kind of looks like we're in a swamp. Or near a swamp. I don't know, I just don't want to be eaten by an alligator before I even turn eighteen, you know?" She reaches up and pushes a lock of dirty-blonde hair behind her ear.

"I doubt they'd have kept us alive this long just to feed us to an alligator," I find myself reassuring her, even though we're on shaky ground right now.

"I hope you're right because that seems like a bad way to go. I remember learning about them in school, and supposedly the infection from their saliva kills you if you live long enough. Usually, they drown you before then." She shudders, wrapped up in the memory.

"Well, that's a delightful thing to know," I mutter under my breath. Just add it to the list of things after us—crazy kidnapping cabal? Check. NLC doctors who want to sedate and impregnate us? Check. Infected alligator spit? Double check.

On the heels of that delightful thought, we trailed out of the room behind Nell to find out our fate.

Two

LOCK AND KEY

We follow behind Nell, Patrick leaning heavily into my shoulders, as we exit the aircraft. The gunmetal-black interior gleams dully before we step out into the dark, and walk down a metal grate gangplank. The heavy heat and humidity are a slap to the face as we reach the bottom of the grating, and I stop to drag in a lungful of air. It's so humid that it actually feels thick in my lungs, a disconcerting sensation. Glancing over at Patrick, I see that, instead of making internal observations of the weather, he's actively scanning our surroundings for danger.

You should probably be paying more attention to that yourself, Sadie. Alligators and all. I force myself to tear my eyes away from Patrick, and try to make out details about where we've landed. The aircraft is giving off very little light, and all I can really make out is dense underbrush and towering trees looming around the small clearing we're standing in.

A tired sigh directly behind us makes me jump, and Patrick winces at the sudden movement.

"Y'all planning to stand here all night, or are we gone' get some rest at some point? This thing ain't gone' fly itself outta here and

8

even the Maverick can't fly in her sleep, y'hear me?" The woman's thick drawl is more resigned than angry. In the dim light it's hard to tell much about her, but I can make out a short, curvy figure in what appears to be a leather jacket.

"Sleep sounds amazing, but we seem to be facing a real shortage of beds at the moment," Nell says in a wry tone, and gestures to the wild surroundings.

"Pssh, you ain't seen nothin' yet. Follow me." She brushes past us, and walks off towards the thick undergrowth. After a beat of awkward indecision, the three of us follow quickly, since she's already fading into the soupy night.

The woman—excuse me—*the Maverick* . . . walks ahead of us with her hands jammed into her pockets, seemingly without a care in the world. After a minute or two, we reach the edge of the clearing and what appeared to be a solid wall of foliage gives way to a miniscule footpath.

"Stay tight with me. Y'all wander into this hea' swamp, the Ol' Man be using your bones for toothpicks before sunup," she says matter-of-factly.

"Err . . . Maverick . . . who's the Old Man?" I dare to ask, the only deviation I can allow myself from keeping my eyeballs trained to the faint sight of her heels on the path ahead of us. Patrick gives my shoulders a light squeeze, and then lurches away from me, to support himself.

"Call me Mav, honey, everybody else does. And shoo' yeah, the Ol' Man. This is his territory. Helena might think she's queen bee, but Ol' Man was here before us, and he'll be here after us. Gators don't mind bees, queen or not. They got tough hide."

Patrick's only response to her astute observation is a snort.

9

The short interlude gives way to quiet, and then again the sounds of the unseen life teeming around us rise up. Insect chirps fill the air first, followed by some sort of call I can't identify, and finally a high-pitched, repetitive noise that causes Maverick to pause and hold up a hand. For a moment we all swat at the cloud of mosquitoes dogging us while Maverick listens carefully to the unfamiliar sound. I snake a hand backwards, and entwine my fingers with Patrick's. His warm grip grounds me in this bizarre situation. *How many more of these are we going to endure before we get to live our lives in peace?*

"Ol' Lady must have hatched a late set this year. Whoo, she gon' be mad we're in her territory." With that ominous comment, she takes off at a faster clip, and we stumble along behind her, the knobby roots causing me to trip more than once into trees with bark that seems to be peeling away under my brief touches.

After a few more minutes of rushed winding along the footpath, the ground seems to smooth out and the path widens, onto a lawn with grasses waving at knee-high. But as we exit the swamp, it's not the grass that pulls my eyes like magnets. Up ahead is the most beautiful old plantation house I've ever seen, its porch lights calling to me with old-world charm.

Along the echoes of an ancient driveway, tall mossy oaks stand proud sentry to our approach, swaying in the night breeze. Stately white columns support a double wrap-around porch, and lights gleam in nearly every burnished window. The sight nearly takes my breath away with relief. No matter who we're with, I know there's a bed in there with my name on it.

Patrick gives my hand a gentle squeeze, and I hastily start forward down the front walk, the ancient trees waving above us in the hot night breeze.

We clamber up the front porch, and a trickle of relief floods my veins at being out of alligator territory, but then a wave of anger follows hot on its heels. I exchange a meaningful glance with Patrick, his jaw set in a hard line as we cross the threshold into the ancient home. *We might be out of the swamp, but that doesn't mean there aren't any predators.*

Nell crowds close to my other side, and we all scan the interior in silence. Before we have time to make it past the foyer, Atlas rounds a corner and strides up to embrace Nell. She sinks into him, and returns the hug.

"I think we need to talk," he says lightly, making eye contact over Nell's dishwater-blonde head.

"Yes, we certainly do," Patrick says coldly.

Atlas jerks his head towards a staircase, and we all follow soundlessly, our footsteps on the creaking stair treads loud in the night. Looking back over my shoulder, I see the Maverick clearly for the first time as she steps across the threshold into the house. She seems to shudder in that moment, before shaking it off and crossing the room with no spare steps. My first impression of her was accurate, as the light reveals a short, curvy black woman with close-cropped kinky curls, and a deep red bomber jacket with a fleece collar.

We arrive at the top of the landing, and Atlas cuts left down a hallway. I don't see another soul up here, and the antique sconces on the wall cast shadows along the wood floors. They gleam as if recently polished, and I wonder for the hundredth time since we landed how this safe house came to be.

At the end of the hallway, Atlas pushes through a doorway without knocking. Inside is a large, well-appointed bedroom. Light, lacy curtains on the windows speak of times gone by, while the gleaming metal I see through the open bathroom door hint at modern comforts.

My mind is quickly distracted from the amenities, as Patrick cuts straight to business. "Atlas, what is going on? Tell me you didn't drop us in the Resistance's lap without our knowledge or consent."

He's silent for a beat, and then gives an arrogant shrug of his shoulder in response. "You wanted out, didn't you?"

My anger, which had been simmering low in my gut, boils over at his unapologetic words. It's as though I'm watching someone else when I cross the two steps between us, pull back my fist, and slam it straight into his too-smug jaw.

"What in the world!" Nell half-shouts.

At the same instant, Patrick barks, "Sadie!"

But I barely hear them, as I'm so focused on Atlas's unruffled expression. Infuriatingly, Atlas barely sways at the impact, and I'm tempted to take another swing. However, what might not have physically moved him did have the desired effect. He tossed up both hands in surrender. "I'm giving you that one, Sadie, since this was a crappy day. Will you let me *explain* before you go for round two, at least?"

Patrick's hand on my arm drags me back to his side, and my hand, still clenched into a tight fist, is trapped against him. Nell flutters at Atlas's side, as if trying to figure out what to do with her hands. Seeing that he's unhurt, she turns wide eyes back to me.

Satisfied that I'm not coming out swinging again, he lowers his hands slowly, and then rubs his jaw and thumbs the edge of his lip, checking for blood. "For a small woman, you pack a lot of temper, you know that?" He pauses, eyeing me thoughtfully. "Are you ready to hear me out now, before you go for the jugular?"

My anger somewhat in check, and curiosity piqued, I nod once.

Nell, wide-eyed at my outburst, interrupts, "Can we sit? I'm exhausted and this doesn't sound like a short story."

Atlas slips a tattooed arm around her shoulders, and leads her to a loveseat against the far wall. We settle into two wing-backed chairs across from them, but I can't relax.

Atlas leans forward, forearms on knees, and dives right into his explanation in a low voice. "Yes, I called the Resistance. No, I did not tell you. No, I had no idea they were going to kidnap us all today. You asked me to find a way out that didn't incriminate us and, despite my connections, there are only two groups that have the ability to pull that off. To my mind, the Resistance might not be *friends*, but they're friendlier than the extremists." He makes eye contact with Patrick, who gives a single, reserved nod for him to continue.

"When I called, they asked for three things; a list of the people we wanted extracted, our schedules for the next two weeks, and a bargaining chip. The price of admittance to the Resistance is something to further the cause. So, I told them about our discovery, and they said they'd get back to me." He spreads his hands wide, tension evident in his broad shoulders. "I had no idea when they were coming, and I certainly didn't expect a full-on abduction with no advance warning. Since I know Helena," he says with a bitter tone, "it's not a complete surprise. She said it would be in the next few weeks, but you and I haven't had any time without company since I placed the pick-up call to fill you in."

Now that he's said his piece, he leans back against the cushion, and falls silent. I churn his words in my mind, parsing it all. Atlas hasn't betrayed us, after all. I don't approve of his having kept us in the dark, but I see that this wasn't entirely his decision. Grudgingly, I turn to Patrick to gauge his opinion on the situation.

He's silent, leaning back in his seat, his dark expression a strange juxtaposition for the dainty floral chair. After a moment he lets out a ragged sigh, and runs a hand through his hair with a weary expression. "So, what now? I assume you had an exit plan when you decided the Resistance was our best way out."

At that, Atlas grins. "Yes and no. I have a plan, but not only for an exit. With the Resistance, we can regroup, get our proof, and make a play to stop this. Here's what I had in mind . . ."

Utterly exhausted by the day we've had, I listen as long as I can to the men's strategizing before I succumb to the sweet lull of sleep. The last thing I see is the first hint of pink on the horizon peeking through the oaks out front, and then darkness consumes me.

THREE

BREAKFAST OF CHAMPIONS

I'm awoken from a dead sleep by movement under my cheek, followed by a tickling sensation of dust in my nose. I sneeze, and then crack open one eye to see bright, mid-day sun pouring in the windows. My next breath fills my nose with the scent of an unfamiliar pillow, and I sit up to see the bathroom door click to a soft close behind Patrick. As the information slowly filters into my exhausted brain, the events of the night before wash over me in a jumble.

Patrick's okay. Atlas didn't betray us. We're with the Resistance. By the time I've caught back up to the present, Patrick walks back into the room.

"Sadie! I'm sorry, I was trying not to wake you up." He smiles that lazy smile of his, and warmth settles in my stomach. No matter what mess we are in the middle of, at least I'm not in it alone. I stand stiffly, and cross the floor to wrap my arms around him. Breathing in his familiar scent, I feel grounded again. It's amazing how quickly this man, and not a location, has become my home.

I lean back, and he brushes a strand of hair back from my face with a gentle touch. "You're so beautiful in the mornings. It's like all of the craziness is washed away in the night, and each day, here we are again and you're so perfect for me. I lo—" His soft murmur is cut off by a swift pounding on the door.

We both turn, the moment ruined. A deep male voice I don't recognize comes through with stern undertones, "Meeting on the back balcony in forty-five minutes. Up and at 'em, sleeping beauties." Terse, heavy bootsteps traverse the hall, and the mystery man repeats the pound-and-deliver-the- message routine at the next room.

Shaking my head, I wander into the bathroom, still drowsy.

Ten minutes later, refreshed from a good tooth brushing and a clean set of borrowed clothes—in all black, of course—we pad down the hallway to the stairs hand in hand. Patrick stops me, and we both listen to the sounds of the house's inhabitants stirring around us. Whatever he was listening for, he's now satisfied, so we step quietly down the stairs, and peer around the stately room. It's well maintained, but lost in time. The decor is heavy and rich, as if from a century gone by. Bright red wallpaper adorns the walls, in one of those endlessly scrolling patterns that gives me a headache.

Patrick leads me through a doorway. "There's got to be a kitchen around here somewhere," he mutters under his breath.

We twist and turn through the large house, and each room is similar to the first—sumptuous, and ancient. Heavy wood furniture with scrollwork detailing, and gently fading brocade fabrics greet us in each room. A shiver crawls down my spine. For a moment, the hot chamber feels as if the former inhabitants are still lingering here, watching us in disapproval.

Finally, we push open a swinging door to find bright, modern overhead lighting and an immaculate sparkling kitchen. There, leaning against a glossy countertop is the Maverick. Her conversation with a man in an apron stops abruptly as we enter.

"Well now, if we don't have Sleeping Beauty and Prince Charming in our midst," she observes in a sarcastic tone before taking a sip from her mug. "Come on in, don't be shy on our account. Do you like coffee? Get yourself a cup. Rex hea' will have breakfast ready in a jiffy."

The smell of coffee permeates the room, and Patrick is already scanning the counters for the coffee maker. He spots it, and crosses to grab a mug and help himself to a cup. I stand awkwardly inside the doorway, watching as Rex turns back to the industrial-sized stove and gets busy cracking eggs. Patrick rejoins me a moment later and lets out a contented sigh after his first sip of coffee.

"This is good, thank you." He takes another hearty swallow.

"None for you, little lady?" Maverick asks.

I shake my head. "No, I don't drink coffee. Thank you, though." The words are barely out of my mouth before Rex procures a glass from a cabinet overhead and pulls a glass pitcher of orange juice from the refrigerator. He fills the glass with a flourish and passes it to me without a word.

"A'right then, why don't we wait outside so we won't be in Rex's hair? He's more of a sole operator than a chatty Cathy." She nods towards the ornate French doors, and we follow her out onto the back porch.

In the daytime, the view is spectacular. More oak trees line the back way, and the lush greenery of the swamp surrounds us while bird calls and amphibian croaks blend with the constant breeze to form a natural soundtrack.

"It's beautiful here," I comment as we walk to the railing.

"Beautiful, and sad too," Mav says in the most solemn tone we've heard from her yet. I follow her gaze, and notice the nearly rotten remains of three smaller, wooden houses towards the tree line that are barely more than a few slumped, shadowy forms after time has wreaked its havoc on them.

"Are those . . . were they slave houses?" I ask, my tone now matching hers.

"M-hmm. It shore is easier to forget the problems of the past, but in my opinion that will just bring 'em back round again, once people forget." She taps her fingers on the intricately carved banister, deep in thought. After a long silence, she continues, "Feels like they are about here, in a way. It's real disturbing, what you all uncovered."

My blood chills at the thought of the women strapped in those beds, years of life stripped from them with their own flesh and blood, and I have to agree with her—it's not the same as the past, but in no way acceptable for the future. Anger rises in me once again and stiffens my resolve. I might not have planned to be here, surrounded by these tepid allies, but at least we're in a better place to act, and to change something.

"We're going to free those women, and we're not going to let history repeat itself." Patrick's voice is insistent. His dedication to my cause makes my heart beat a little faster in appreciation.

How did I get so lucky?

"You're a'right, you know that?" Mav looks over at him and gives him a cocky half-grin. "For a rich boy, anyways."

We all chuckle at her not-so-subtle dig, but before he can respond, the French doors open and we all turn to see Helena and Brock walk out onto the balcony like they're storming enemy territory. "Good morning, everyone." Helena speaks first, tone icy. "Or afternoon, for the rest of us."

Ahh, nothing like a condescending overlord to get your blood pumping in the morning. Oh, excuse me—afternoon. I roll my eyes internally but keep the sarcasm to myself.

Patrick, ever the diplomat, answers without any ruffled feathers, "Good afternoon to you, Helena, Brock. This is a beautiful safe house, and we appreciate your hospitality."

Brock's only response is a slight incline of his head before he takes a seat at the long picnic-style table at the end of the veranda. Helena sits next to him and gestures for the three of us to follow.

"Everyone else is on their way up, and Rex is nearly finished preparing the food. We'll make it a working brunch, so we can move on to phase two."

As if on cue, the doors open again and a stream of black-clad Resistance members pour out onto the porch, trailed by Atlas and, finally, Nell, rubbing sleep from her eyes and giving me a bleary look as she settles into the heavy chair next to me.

"Oh, where did Patrick get coffee?" she asks on an exhale. "I would kill for some coffee."

"Rex had a pot going in the kitchen," Patrick tells her with a small smile.

"I don't suppose you'd just give me that cup, would you?"

"Not a chance." He smirks and takes a long swallow.

"I'll be right back." Her grumpy tone says it all, but she manages not to slam the door on her way back into the house.

While most groups of this size would chatter, everyone sits in silence, and once again the eerie resonance of the wind through the trees offers the only break in the silence.

After an extended pause, Helena claps twice to get everyone's attention, and jumps right to the point. "Okay, everyone, great work yesterday with the extraction. Today's a new day, however, and there's new work to be done. We'll be setting up our four newest members"—she glances at us dismissively as she talks—"in a family home on the west side of the compound. There's less foot traffic there, and we're hoping they can stay out of the limelight. Since you won't all be needed for that, half of you will be staying here awaiting the transport to the next job." She gestures to Mav, who inclines her head in acknowledgement that she'll be ferrying them around. "Brock will hand out the assignments." She runs a hand down Brock's bicep possessively, and the sight bothers me for some reason.

"Karin, Leo, and James, you'll be on their security detail in the compound—" Brock rattles off names efficiently, and I zone out almost immediately. In all likelihood, I'll never see half of these people again after today.

Nell slides back into the chair next to me, and the smell of coffee assaults my nose, making my stomach churn angrily. *What is it with the smells lately? Ugh.*

"What'd I miss?" she asks under her breath.

"Nothing yet.Just splitting up the security detail so far," I answer in a hushed tone. I can't help but lean away from the offending mug, and bump Patrick's arm. He gives me a quick kiss on the top of the head, and then focuses back on Brock. I try to focus too, and ignore my angry stomach. *It'll get better once I've had some breakfast.*

"Okay, we've decided to keep things simple to set you four up as a poly-family. That way, there won't be any questions, and nobody is going to think you're who you are, since they would never suspect the new prince and princess of the NAA to be joining us. To make matters better, though, we need to alter your appearance a bit. Since you're clean shaven, we ask that you grow a beard. And ladies, you'll need to alter your appearances as well. How do you feel about colored contacts?" She looks down her nose at us, and I simply shrug in response. If it keeps us safe, I'll do it. I I don't give two cow patties what color my eyes are.

Nell raises her hand, like a kid in school. Helena rolls her eyes, and answers archly, "Yes?"

"What is a poly-family, exactly?"

I forgot Nell hadn't already gotten the rundown on this from Pierce, like I had back at the NLC. "A poly-family is any familial grouping involving three or more adults." Her tone is crisp, as if daring Nell to object.

Nell raises one eyebrow, and asks cautiously, "And this is . . . *common* where you live? I didn't think that was legal." She looks at Atlas, but he just slips an arm on the back of her chair around her shoulders in lieu of a response.

Brock sighs in annoyance. "You really think any way of living outside the NAA's rule is legal, Nell? Would we be in the middle of this god-forsaken nowhere swamp at a safe house if you were allowed to live where you wanted and marry who you wanted? No. *Think.*"

Nell leans back, as if slapped by the outburst of irritation from this near-stranger. Her eyes narrow and she starts to lean forward again, the retort clear in her gaze when Atlas shifts to put a subtle hand on her shoulder.

"You'll have to forgive us Brock, none of us have had time to debrief on the situation, given the rather abrupt method you chose for extraction." His sarcasm rings clear in the morning, and Brock's jaw ticks in anger.

"Would you like to go back, because that could be arranged just as abruptly—" he points an accusing finger at Atlas, but is interrupted from his building tirade by Rex pushing through the balcony doors.

"Grub's up. Can I get a few hands to bring it all out?" He drops a platter of bacon with a clang to the middle of the table, and a few members of the security team rise and follow him back in.

Helena cuts in before the men have a chance to take the argument up another notch. "Brock, I don't think she meant any judgement. She's young, and new to our lifestyle. I'm sure once they see the compound, they'll understand."

He still looks bristly, but his shoulders unclench at her words, and he lets it drop.

Throughout the entire exchange, I was riveted to my seat, and only the wafting smell of bacon and the abrupt end of the conversation frees me from watching the back and forth. Patrick reaches across me to the platter, and drops two pieces onto the white plate in front of me, and two on his own.

I chuckle. "In a hurry, Mr. O'Roarke? There's enough bacon there to feed an army."

He shrugs without apology. "Sure, but in case you didn't notice, we're sitting with a small army. You snooze, you lose." He punctuates the sentiment by taking off half a piece in one bite. He gestures to my plate, and I grab a piece to take a nibble.

The savory flavor is delicious, but doesn't sit well in my stomach. I set it back down, and hear a rumbling noise behind us. Turning, I see a dusty white van bumping out of the woods over uneven ground, and heading straight towards us.

"Uhm, Patrick . . . that's not the NAA, is it?" My hand tightens on his arm in reflexive fear.

"Of course not," Helena snaps. "It's the last member of your party." She gives a vague gesture down to the rear yard where a side door opens, and a short, bespectacled man with unruly hair tumbles out, and then promptly vomits into the bushes.

The sound nearly makes me do the same, but, thankfully, he stops quickly and wipes his mouth. When he turns toward the porch where we're all sitting and raises a hand in cheerful greeting, we see it's none other than Glitch.

FOUR

CALIVADA

There is a new urgency in the air, and the breakfast platters are dropped without fanfare on the table after Helena announces we're leaving in thirty minutes. Glitch is brought in and we all rise and hug him, after which he sits at the end of the table and sips a cup of coffee. He fills us in on his own abduction while we eat as much as we can hold, which unfortunately for me isn't all that much before it's time to leave for the next leg of our trip.

Helena has barely risen from the table when something strikes me. "Wait! Helena, what happened to Peter? Glitch is here; the four of us are all here. Where's Peter? Is he okay?"

Her brow furrows for a moment in confusion, and she turns to Brock, who answers instead. "Peter, the police captain? I believe he was left incapacitated at the scene. Well, assuming he wasn't dead," he adds with a shrug, and I feel my insides start to boil, as I rise from the table.

"What do you mean, assuming he wasn't dead? How is that even a question?" My voice rises in pitch, and it sounds shrill even to me.

"Listen, little girl, when we have a target to pull, that's our main priority. I'm sorry if you got overly attached to your head of security, but based on your reaction it sounds like we did your *husband* a favor." He takes a dismissive swig of his coffee, clearly considering the conversation closed.

You arrogant son of a —

My thoughts blur into an unintelligible haze of anger. Without a second thought, I pick up my almost-full glass of orange juice and toss it directly into his smug face.

"That man you dismissed as just another NAA police captain was my *brother* and I'd appreciate it if you didn't treat his life as collateral damage! Now, how the hell would he be dead, if one of your men wasn't to blame?!"

His face pure thunderclouds, Brock rises so slowly from his seat it feels like I'm watching an ancient mountain rise from the sea. By the time he straightens to his full height, my neck is craned back to look up at him, but I don't care one whit, and I don't back off.

"How. Dare. You. You five troublemakers are here on our good graces, and you have the *audacity* to throw a drink in my face? I ought to load you all up and have Mav drop you in the swamp!" He yells so loudly that a flock of cranes takes flight from the nearest clump of trees.

Patrick is on his feet in half a second, arm stretched in front of me in defense. "I think you need to calm down, Brock, and remember that you shouldn't speak to my wife with anything less than respect."

Helena reaches up and places a hand on his broad shoulder, but his gaze never strays from mine, and the sneer on his lips tells me exactly what he thinks of me.

I don't care, you heartless bastard. I'm not scared of you.

"I'm sure we can have one of our people follow up and get a status update on your brother, Sadie. That wasn't in the file, so we weren't aware of the familial connection." Helena's voice is even and diplomatic, but the truth is in Brock's hate-filled eyes. These people may be temporary allies, but it's not our best interest they've got at heart; it's their own. And I won't forget it.

"Yes, Helena, please do. I think we'll wait out front for our transport." Atlas's voice from my other shoulder startles me, but it's reassuring to see him on his feet too, looking menacing at my right shoulder. A gaze around the end of the table shows Glitch and Nell right behind him, also up and looking affronted on my behalf.

They may be new friends, but they're real friends. I think to myself as we walk out the door. I can hear furious, hushed whispers behind us as we cross back into the kitchen, but I don't care. My heart is heavy, wondering about Peter. *Please be okay, Peter. I'll never forgive myself if you aren't.*

The trip to the Resistance compound in Calivada was not a pleasant one. After our confrontation at the breakfast table, Brock apparently decided to be petty, and only have Mav fly us to the nearest way station. After she dropped the five of us off, we were met by a small white van, similar to the one that dropped off Glitch, and with none of the luxurious extras the NLC flaunted at every turn.

The following hours were cramped, hot, and filled with stops to let Glitch out to vomit on the side of the road. Each time we stopped, my stomach tried to crawl up my throat in commiseration with his. As a result, I skipped lunch completely besides sipping a cold soda. Patrick looked concerned, but let it pass when I begged off.

Now, finally, as the sun's about to set, the driver lets us know that we'll be pulling into the compound momentarily, and we're all looking out the windows with renewed interest. We come around a bend and are greeted by a gate set in an over-large stone wall. It extends as far as the eye can see ahead of us, and I'm shocked by the sheer size of the thing.

How is this here—and this huge—outside of NAA reach? It's a question I'll have to save for Patrick later. He didn't seem thrilled to be with the Resistance, so I'm sure he's got information on it, if I can stay awake long enough to hear it tonight.

The van driver pulls up to a massive, camera-studded gate, lists his name and credentials, and removes his glasses for the nearest camera. A moment later we hear the whine of a motor and the gate inches backwards at a snail's pace. Once it opens, the driver zips through and proceeds down a twisty driveway at a much too rapid clip. I try to focus on the clumps of sawgrass lining the driveway—and not my heaving stomach—but, after two minutes, my mouth starts to water unpleasantly and I can't take it any more.

"Stop the van, please! I'm going to be sick." I yell before covering my mouth. My belly starts to heave before we're fully stopped, and I yank the sliding door open and stumble out. I barely miss tripping into a large, sharp-leafed plant before I retch up the half sandwich I'd eaten at our last stop. The nausea is gone almost as fast as it appeared, and my awareness of my surroundings finally returns. Patrick's warm hand on my back is both comforting and mortifying, given what he just witnessed. Before I can comment, he presses a napkin into my hand, and kisses me on the temple.

"One second, Sadie. I'll get you something to rinse your mouth out." He half-jogs to the back of the van, and gets a water bottle and a lemon-lime soda from the cooler in the back. I can still see the last broken pieces of ice sliding free when he hands me the water.

After a good swish, I feel much better, and thoroughly embarrassed by the audience for my moment of illness.

"Better now?" Patrick asks with a smile, and I fall just a bit more in love with him as I take in the crinkle at the corner of his eyes, and the kindness in his gaze.

I nod in response, and the burn of embarrassment in my cheeks starts to fade.

"Good," he says, brushing a piece of dark hair back from my face. "You look a little pale. What do you say we walk the rest of the way? We're only about a half mile away, and the fresh air will probably feel better than getting back into the van. But, it's up to you."

I can't contain my shudder at the idea of getting back into the van. "Yes, a walk sounds great."

Without another word, he leads me gently by the hand to the driver's door, whose window is rolled down. "We'll walk the rest of the way. Which house is ours?"

"You're in 1712."

"Thanks, man."

With a wave, the driver speeds off into the falling night, and I'm grateful to be off the wild ride.

We walk hand-in-hand, unhurried, down the gravel drive. For a moment it feels as if we're any two people on a lover's stroll. The breeze is balmy, the tang of salt in the air confirms my suspicion that we've come nearly to the Pacific Ocean and, just for now, it feels like everything is going to be okay.

Eventually, Patrick breaks the silence. "Sadie, I want to ask you something, but I don't want you to feel . . . well, I don't know. Pressured? Upset? I'm—actually, I'm not even sure how to ask, but—" He stops and runs a hand through his perfectly floppy hair.

Rather than let him stew, I cut to the point I know he's trying to make. "Patrick, I think I might be pregnant."

A surprising amount of fear at speaking the words aloud runs through my veins, spiking my heart rate. *How is he going to react? Is he going to be happy? He didn't look happy to be asking,* I think warily, the thoughts bouncing in my head almost as quickly as my heart is pounding in my chest.

He stops dead in his tracks, and turns to face me.

"Do you really think so? I mean, there was that announcement right before we left, but we never found out what it was. It could have been anything, but we have no way of knowing now."

Here it is, the moment of truth. "Well, there's no way to be sure, but I think it's possible. We'd have to get a test to confirm it, but I've been feeling—"

The rest of the sentence is lost to the fabric of his black t-shirt as he pulls me into a fierce hug. All I can do is hug him back, the lump in my throat preventing any further conversation. I don't know how long we stay like that, clinging to each other for dear life on the side of the driveway, but it is an eternity and not long enough in the same heartbeat.

When we were both ready, he slowly eases back from the hug, and reaches up to cup my chin in his hand, as if I am made of porcelain he is afraid to crack. One reverent swipe of his thumb across my cheek is followed by another. His deep blue eyes are shining when he finally speaks, "I love you so much, Sadie. You're going to be a wonderful mother, and I can't wait to raise this baby with you."

His words bring my tears on full force, and I struggle to hold them back so I can speak coherently what's in my heart. "I love you too, Patrick. But I'm so scared. We're not settled, we're surrounded by people who want to use us for their own ends, and there's no clear path in sight for us, for this baby." My hands drop to my abdomen without thought, and in the back of my mind I'm amazed at how quickly the instinct has kicked in to protect this maybe-there baby of ours.

His expression turns fierce, eyebrows drawn down. "Sadie, I promise you that I will not let anything happen to you, or our baby. We will figure this out—and if we can't find a path forward, we'll make our own. We can do this—*together*."

My heart clenches at his sincerity, and I crumple back into his chest. He wraps his arms around me, and holds me in his comforting embrace. Tomorrow, I'll be strong. Tomorrow, I'll figure out how to get a test and find out if my suspicions are right. Tomorrow, I'll be the determined, take-no-prisoners woman who is being hunted by all and sundry. But today—today I'm just me, in this moment with my husband—and I wouldn't have it any other way.

The next morning's dawn finds us in a new house, in an over-large bed, in an unfamiliar room with orange walls. The glare of the new sun off of the orange paint is biting into my eyes when Patrick's gentle shake rouses me.

"Ugh." I grumble, and roll to cover my head with the pillow.

"Sadie, it's time to wake up. Nell made breakfast, and our guards are supposed to give us a tour in half an hour."

"I don't care about a tour." His chuckle penetrates my pillow, and I'm annoyed. "Aren't we supposed to be in hiding? Why are they parading us around?" I fire back the questions, but my ridiculously chipper husband doesn't mind. *Curse him and his eternal morning happiness.*

My pillow disappears, and I sit bolt upright, ready to give Patrick what-for, but I freeze, my stomach a churning mess of *ick.*

"Sadie, are you all right?" Patrick asks, voice laced with concern. "You don't look so good—"

I don't hear the rest of his sentence, as I bolt to the turquoise-walled bathroom and swing the door forcefully shut behind me. I barely make it to the toilet before the dry heaves start. And go on for what feels like ten years.

Eventually my stomach sends the signal to my brain that it's done heaving, and I sit back on my heels in misery. A timid knock at the door draws my attention. "Sadie, are you okay? Can I get you anything? Maybe some toast, or eggs? Orange juice?"

Patrick's helpful suggestions make my stomach squeeze in anticipation. *Not the good kind.* "No! No food. Do we have any of that lemon soda? Or ginger ale?" I slowly haul myself off the floor, wipe my face with a cool rag, and wash up. Feeling slightly more human, I pull open the door and Patrick nearly falls through the doorway, from his hovering. His handsome, tanned face is creased with worry.

"Sadie, you need to eat something. And we *really* need to get our hands on a test."

I sigh, and lean my forehead against his shoulder. "Patrick, I love you, but it's too early for this. I will take a piece of toast, and some lemon soda. The rest of it can wait." Shuffling back over to the bed, I ignore his expression of protest and sink back to the mattress with a grateful sigh.

"I think we can postpone the tour. I'll be right back with the toast." He kisses me gently on the forehead, and I thank my lucky stars that he's a reasonable man.

The toast turns out to be not so bad, and lemon-lime soda, Lim-Eze, was clearly sent straight from heaven on a unicorn made of rainbows. Because after the first sip, I feel human again, and by the last sip, I'm back to my usual, cranky morning self.

Good to the last drop. "We need to buy this stuff in bulk," I say earnestly as I pass Patrick the empty can before we leave our room.

Nell is waiting anxiously in the living room, and she doesn't waste any time before blurting what she's thinking. "Are you pregnant? Because Atlas is worried . . ." She thinks better of it, and bites her bottom lip.

I fiddle anxiously with the end of my braid. Do I tell her my suspicion? We're all living together, so if this morning is any indication of how things are going to go, it won't be a secret for long. "Atlas is worried, what?" I counter, keeping things vague.

"Atlas is worried that there isn't enough security here if you're pregnant. It would make you a much more valuable target to pretty much everyone who's after you."

My stomach, happy for such a brief minute, feels like I swallowed a boulder instead of a piece of dry toast. "I don't know, Nell." I pause, swallow, and force myself to continue. "But, I think so." I hate how small my voice sounds with the confession, but I don't have it in me to say it any other way.

Nell's eyes well with instant tears, and I brace myself for a meltdown. Instead, she nearly knocks me over with the force of her unexpected hug. "That's amazing, Sadie. I'm so happy for you."

I can't help but smile, and squeeze her back equally hard. "Well, we don't know anything for sure, yet. We need to find a way to confirm without telling everybody and their brother."

"We also now have a firm deadline for getting out of here. Nine weeks, give or take." Atlas's voice from their bedroom doorway startles Nell and me apart.

"Why nine weeks?" Nell asks.

"We need to be long gone before you start to show. The Resistance may be harboring us for now, but you're carrying the heir to the entire NAA, and that's a bargaining chip too good to pass up. We can keep the morning sickness under wraps under the guise of staying out of sight, but if anyone starts to suspect, we have to leave."

Patrick speaks up next. "I agree, but I'd feel more comfortable if we made that seven. Sadie's going to need medical care, and that's hard to arrange without clueing in the doctor."

"Guys, we still don't know that I'm pregnant," I point out, but nobody bats an eye at my weak assertion.

"Didn't you two take pregnancy classes at the NLC? Surely they taught you the signs," Atlas says dryly, and it is with utter glee that I watch Nell march over to him with a hand on her hip and stare him down.

"Atlas, so far I have taken you for a smart man. You could prove it to me by shutting up any time now." Her voice brooks no argument, and I'm surprised to see him look abashed at the reprimand. I'm even more surprised when the mountain of a man doesn't say another word. Instead, Nell turns and takes over.

"I'm sure they've got a pregnancy testing program. I'll tell them I'm due for my testing cycle, and go from there. Nobody's going to care if I'm pregnant, and it won't put us in any danger." She nods once, sharply, as if approving of her own plan, then turns back to me. "Are you ready for a quick tour?"

"After you, boss-lady," I say with a smile.

She chuckles, but doesn't argue as she leads the way out the front door of our shared home.

FIVE

A PRINCESS IN THE STREETS

Nell is still smiling when she flings open the front door, startling the two loitering guards. They stiffen at our sudden appearance, and the dirty-blonde on the left raises his bushy eyebrow before commenting, "Someone under the weather this morning?" His eyes dart back and forth between the grinning Nell, and me where I stand behind her, fidgeting with the dark tendrils at the end of my braid. When neither of us comments after a lengthy pause, he shrugs and looks at his darker-complexioned cohort for direction.

Mr. Tall and Dark wastes no time getting to brass tacks. "All right. Helena debriefed us this morning on the plan for your stay with us. For the time being, you four will be presented as a new quad from up around Manisas. The arrival of an already formed quad may raise a few eyebrows, but we're banking on the likelihood that curiosity is *less* dangerous to your cover than people trying to joining your relationship." He taps his chin thoughtfully, as if that was all perfectly clear, before adding, "Although, they still may, given you have two women."

The nausea must be making me slow this morning, because Patrick beats me to the question at hand, "What's a quad, exactly?"

Bushy Brows sighs, and flops back against the column supporting our small paved porch. The impact from his meaty frame causes a slight tremor, and I distractedly look at the porch ceiling before focusing back on the more serious of our guards.

". . . essentially, the four of you together in a committed relationship." He ticks off on his fingers as he explains. "Here we've got mostly quints, quads, triads, and standard couples—not many, but a few. And here and there, a bachelor who hasn't committed to anyone yet. That's how Glitch has been set up in the bachelor block of the compound." He gives a vague wave over his left shoulder where more rows of small houses stretch uniformly towards the wall. "Most people come in as bachelors or couples, but they don't stay that way for long."

Bushy Brows snorts, but doesn't look away from the point he's staring at on the porch ceiling.

Nell wrinkles her nose at his matter-of-fact dialogue, but I elbow her. "You can't act grossed out, Nell. No one is going to believe we belong here if you give them all side-eye."

"Well, I better get it out now. It seems gross. And weird." She pauses for a moment. "And won't the kids be confused? I mean, I only had my aunt and uncle, and that was bad enough. Imagine having *five* adults in your life." She shudders delicately. It's no surprise to me that her thoughts immediately go to the kids in the families, based on what I've surmised about her bad childhood.

I reach over and give her hand a reassuring squeeze. "Nell, let's just try to be open-minded. We won't be here for long, and even if we don't understand these peoples' choices, we're fighting for *everyone* to be free, right?"

She sighs. "Right. It's still weird, though. Like, super-duper weird."

"It is different . . . very different." My mind goes back to the shock I felt the first time I was introduced to the idea by Pierce back at the NLC. *It feels like a different lifetime.*

"Can we get on with it? The sooner they're out there, the sooner we get this phase over with," Bushy Brows complains from his spot by the column.

"Branch, would you chill out?" The level-headed guard snaps, before fishing a pair of glasses out of a black tactical pocket. He hands them to Patrick. "We're hopeful that the bruising will be enough to disguise you for now, and then growing out your hair and beard, combined with the glasses and the new relationship status"—he gestures at the four of us—"should be enough to stop people putting the pieces together. Not everyone here saw your introductory TV special."

"Uhm, what about me?" I ask, feeling awkward. "I may not be the prince of the NAA, but we were both on TV."

He smiles almost apologetically. "Well, we've discussed that too. You look quite different in your uniform than the dolled-up princess portrayed on the screen. Between the hair and makeup and the glitzy duds, we don't think it's likely you'll be recognized by the crowd here. *However*, they would still like to dye your hair to be on the safe side."

I grip my thick braid in shock, and glance at Patrick and Nell in turn. "My hair? But I've never dyed it before. I *like* my hair color." The dark mahogany color may not be the most exciting, but it is *mine*, dang it. My jaw ticks in annoyance.

"Oh, no. That's her stubborn face," Patrick mutters under his breath. When I narrow my eyes at him he tries to look innocent, but that ship has sailed.

"Sorry, but you can ask them to keep it subtle, I guess." He gives a one-shoulder shrug. "Boss's orders." Without waiting around for further arguments, he turns on his heel and walks off to the right, toward the center of the compound.

Silently stewing, I follow behind him with my eyes burrowing into the back of his neck. Patrick's hand resting lightly on my shoulder distracts me from my mental tirade, and I glance at his sympathetic expression.

"I'm sorry about your hair, Sadie," he says simply.

So direct, this husband of mine. *I think I'll keep him.* "Thank you," I grit out, but I'm not letting this one go easily. *Stupid Helena.*

Before I can get far into my mental tirade against the indifferent leader in question, the tinkling sound of laughter pulls my attention towards a side street to our left.

I stop, my jaw going slack at the sight. Recovering slightly, I whack Patrick on the arm. "Patrick, look!"

He rubs his arm as he pivots to take in the scene. "Wow. That's just . . . wow."

"Why'd you two stop?" Nell steps up to my other side, before following the direction of our gazes. "Oh, kids! How awesome. That's . . . a *lot* of kids, actually."

Atlas comments in a hushed tone, "Look, is that a set of twins?"

What has to be a group of at least ten kids are kicking a soccer ball back and forth, taking advantage of the quiet side street for an impromptu game. At present, a young boy of four or five has the ball, and as we watch it is clear he doesn't know quite what to do with it. A set of older siblings are explaining something to him from

38

where they bracket him on either side. The girl's wild gestures capture his attention, and her brother hops back and forth from foot to foot, as if to bounce something between his feet.

After a moment, the curly-headed four-year-old screws his face up tight with determination, and hauls off and kicks it with every bit of strength he possesses—which, it turns out, is considerable. The ball sails through the air and bounces off the side of Atlas's head with a merry thwack.

Despite the blow, Atlas doesn't get angry; he just laughs, a deep, rolling sound. Catching the ball before it goes wide, Atlas gently tosses it back to the young boy. "Good kick, buddy."

The child, eyes wide with terror at having smacked the mountain of a man, snatches the ball when it rolls to a stop in front of him, turns, and bolts. All of the kids high tail it after him down the street.

The girl twin stops at the end briefly, and turns to holler back at us, "Thanks, mister!" before she, too, disappears from sight.

Ninety minutes and much haggling with a stylist later, I'm staring into a mirror at my new hairstyle with a frown on my face. The long bangs sweeping down to either side of my face aren't a bad addition, all things considered, but the newly-bleached section at the front makes me look, well, different.

It's a small thing, but it's yet another piece of my identity that's been chipped away. *It's not forever.* Nell stands over my left shoulder, hair unmolested.

"I thought it was going to be ugly at first, I'm not gonna lie, but I actually kind of like it. It makes you look . . . distinguished. It's a striking style. Especially with the green contacts." She strikes a ridiculous pose to illustrate her point, with one shoulder back and her chin held high.

"As soon as we're out of here, I'm dying it back. Also, the contacts itch," I grumble, but I really do appreciate her attempt at encouragement, so I give her a small smile. Trying to push it out of my mind and pretend my hair is the same as usual, we step back out into the street. Unlike the empty quiet first thing this morning, noise pulls our attention from almost every direction when we step out of the salon. An electric transport vehicle buzzes by, piled high with what may be turnips, but it zips off so quickly I can't tell. As the blue lights fade into the distance, raised voices draw my attention across the street.

"Halle, why are you being this way? I swear, ever since I joined the guard unit you've been impossible to live with. Don't you realize we need guards? How do you think our people stay safe? I have a responsibility to step up!"

"Of course I do—I'm not a child! But we already lost Danny. Now you go off and sign up, and what am I supposed to do here alone with three kids when you go, too? Hmm? Did you even think about your responsibility to your own family?"

"You're *all* I think about, Halle. And what am I supposed to say except if I don't join, who will? Every single guard in the NLC has a woman waiting at home!"

"Oh, so I'm just another woman. I see," Halle says, tone dripping bitterness. "In that case, you shouldn't have much trouble finding a different one to sleep next to this evening." She delivers the cut before turning sharply on her heel, and leaves him fuming in her wake. She's a tiny woman, but she's all spark.

He watches her in silence, jaw ticking as she strides down the street. He spins, and at first I think he's going to punch something, but instead he sinks onto a bench in front of the shop, and drops his head into his hands.

My stomach is in knots after watching the scene.

Mr. Tall and Dark—*Ajax*, I correct myself, remembering the stylist's greeting for him—clears his throat, breaking all of us from the frozen trance we've fallen into. "Okay, sorry to give you no down time this morning, but there is a planning meeting that starts in six minutes. If you'll follow me, we'll get you to it." With a swift wave to the stricken man across the street, he leads us farther into the city.

"Okay, fine, I get it, we need to plan. But is there going to be breakfast at some point in this day? Because you can't plan on an empty stomach," Nell grumbles.

Patrick chuckles. "That's usually your line, Sadie." The glare I level on him doesn't phase him in the slightest. "I'm only teasing." He leans in to whisper against my ear. "Besides, I don't want you getting nauseous again. Some food on your stomach should help."

I give him a quiet nod in response, feeling oddly subdued about the entire thing. My brain is too overloaded to worry over any particular piece of the tangle we're in the middle of. I blame the pre-occupation for nearly running into the broad back stopped in front of me. I'm a half second too late to stop, and I stumble and catch myself on his arm.

"Oh, gosh! I'm so sorry. I wasn't looking, and I didn't see you there. Are you okay?" I babble, and look up to striking and familiar crystalline blue eyes. Shock washes through me, even though it shouldn't. After all, Pierce is the reason I knew about this place to begin with.

"Sadie! Wow, I heard you were here, but I didn't expect to see you so soon. Okay—ever." He leans down, and gracefully presses a kiss to my cheek.

Flustered at running into him, I blush furiously. "Hi, Pierce. I didn't expect to see you, either. I mean, what are the odds? This place is pretty huge."

Patrick sticks his hand out to shake, giving me a second to collect my thoughts. "Hey, man. Good to see you."

They shake, and I'm pleased to see there's no animosity, or misplaced competition evident between them.

"Nice to see you again, too."

"Pierce, darling!" As the feminine voice cuts through the line of people slowly making their way into the headquarters, my stomach turns.

People part in a wave as she walks over and smacks a possessive kiss on Pierce's mouth, uncaring about the crowd surrounding them. "Took you long enough, what's keeping you this morning?" She turns a glower in my direction. "I hope our new arrivals haven't caused you any trouble. Shall I introduce you?"

Helena. Pierce's Helena, who he didn't want to give up for a match with me. Shock floods my system. What are the odds?

"No, Hellie. I already know them, remember? Sadie and I were matched at one point," Pierce responds flatly, not rising to the irritation in her tone.

"Oh, yes. How could I possibly forget? Well, do get a move on. We've got lots to discuss." She wraps a red-nailed hand around his tightly and leads him through the parted crowd into the building.

"That is . . . unexpected. But we should keep moving—we're drawing attention." Atlas observes quietly.

Resisting the urge to shake my head at the weirdness of it all, I continue forward, gripping Patrick's hand tightly. He's right, and all of the people waiting to enter the building in their matching black fatigues are staring at us. I'll have to process later, because right now it's time to find out our next steps with the Resistance—and how to get out of Dodge.

SIX

WAR ROOM

T he inside of the Resistance headquarters is both everything and nothing that I expected. A sort of ordered chaos prevails, with men and women in black clustered around the room, some laughing, some arguing. All adding to the overwhelming din bouncing around the metallic walls.

I stop directly inside the door, and Nell steps up to my other side. Leaning in, she whispers, "Holy bananas, this place is a madhouse."

"Yes, it is. I wonder if it's always like this, or if something's happened?" I turn to Patrick, and he shrugs one shoulder.

"I guess we'll find out if they decide to tell us."

Atlas snorts, but stays silent, eyes scanning the room in a continual sweep.

"Look at my man over there, such a hottie. I have a thing for the strong, silent type." Nell practically drools on my shoulder.

"Nell, seriously? Look around. So not the time or place."

She sighs wistfully. "Speak for yourself. It's always the time and place." He looks over, catches her staring, and she gives him a saucy wink.

"This way. The meeting's about to start." Ajax waves us forward, through the middle of the building, and Branch of the Bushy Brows trails behind. As we press through the clusters of people, snatches of conversation assault me.

". . . saying, the king has been on NAA One daily . . ."

"—*Potential!* There's no way we can let this chance pass us by, we won't get . . ."

"Critically low reserves. This isn't a problem that can wait to be addressed in two weeks. Helena has to hear us out today."

That last is from a stern woman, right outside the tall glass door where Ajax stops. Her hair is pulled back in a severe bun, and her features are etched with concern.

"Mari, relax! We'll figure it out," the woman next to her soothes.

"Ladies, good to see you both, as always." Ajax nods cordially as he opens the door for us to enter. The conference room is long and narrow, one side made up of the silvery building wall, and the rest, floor to ceiling glass walls. A skinny cylinder sits at one end of the long, black table. Helena sits at the far end, tapping her fingers impatiently, and looking between Brock and Pierce with a scowl.

Patrick pulls out a chair for me right inside the door, as far from her as we can get while still being in the room. A short stream of others trails in behind us, many of the faces familiar from our "rescue" flight, but not all. Ajax stands behind us against the glass wall, arms crossed tightly against his chest.

Once everyone who wants a seat has one, he reaches over and shuts the door with a solid thump. The sound causes my throat to tighten, but I try not to overanalyze the feeling. *Stay in the moment, Sadie.*

Helena leans forward and taps something on the cylindrical device in front of her, and the glass walls surrounding us instantly

45

fog, decorating itself with a pixelated pattern that reminds me of music notes.

"Let's get this show on the road. Who wants to go first?" she says, sounding bored.

Voices clamor from around the table, but a tall thin man across from us stands, and everyone else quiets. "We are seeing a high number of riots breaking out across the NAA based on the news reports this week, from Playa Reino all the way up to the Alaska Territories. We've been monitoring the situation for now, but we feel that it's in our best interest to begin influencing the outbreaks. This is an opportunity we can't afford to let pass by." His gaze settles on the four of us, and a shiver runs up my spine.

Not friends—simply temporary allies. I remind myself. *Temporary.* Patrick's hand settles on my knee under the table, and he gives me a small squeeze of reassurance. Tilting my head ever so slightly, I see his calm, unruffled expression. If I didn't know better, I'd think he was watching a boring movie, not sitting in a room full of his father's enemies. *Our enemies, eventually.*

"The king has been on NAA One daily since the grab, giving updates on the search for his lost son and daughter-in-law." The chill up my back turns to ice. "Apparently, the public don't like their newly-minted prince being snatched so soon after they got to meet him. As a result, there have been complete losses in two tri-states of the main government buildings, and the NAA Police have been dispatched to restore order in both cases. The rest of the riots haven't proceeded to that point—yet." He sinks gracefully back to his seat, but his eyes don't leave us.

"Thank you, Ryker. We'll take it under advisement. Who's next?" She continues tapping on the table, and the small repetitive noise is beginning to grate on my nerves.

It's the woman from outside the meeting room who pipes up next. "Me, Helena. Our supply situation has become absolutely critical. Our run last week was diverted, to prepare for the pickup. After the failed run two weeks prior, we've got to have a successful run within the next ten days, or we're in deep trouble."

"How deep, Marigold?"

The woman flinches. Whether it's the question or her full name that offends her, I can't tell, but never have I seen a woman who looks less like a Marigold than this stern, pale woman. "Well, we haven't been this low on food reserves since the drought three years ago. And our medical supplies are at less than ten percent, after the injuries treated in the past month. As for birthing kits, we only have two left." She rambles the statistics off by memory, and Helena stiffens at the last.

Hissing through her teeth, Helena reaches forward again, taps a few times on the cylinder, and this time the table in front of us transforms. In front of each of us, a roster of names, ages, and dates appears. It appears to be a list of six women, followed by three more in another section below.

"Two birth kits is unacceptable. I want this remediated within seven days, tops. I am not going to tell any of these women that we're not prepared to support them, are we clear?" There's a long pause, as the innocuous list takes on new meaning. "I trust you'll make it happen?"

Mari nods once, and drops back to her chair.

"Let's get straight to the matter at hand. With us today are Patrick and Sadie Royce, heirs apparent of the entire NAA. In addition we have Atlas and Nell, head of personal security for the Royces."

The silence in the room is complete, save the faint hum of an air conditioning unit. After a weighty pause, she continues.

"I'm bringing it to the table for open discussion. The Royces and their security detail confirmed first hand some of the nefarious acts perpetrated against women by the NAA. How do we get proof? And how do we ensure that those responsible are held accountable?" Her gaze hardens, and she tries to pin Patrick to the chair, as if he's personally responsible.

I bristle at the accusation in her eyes, but Patrick remains calm, and gives my knee a gentle stroke with his thumb as acknowledgement, but nothing more.

Atlas is the first to break the silence, unconcerned with our outsider status. "We already know what we need to do, Helena. It's more a matter if your people will work with us, or not. We witnessed firsthand more than ten pregnant women, sedated, and held in captivity in a facility local to our NAA resort location. With help from our technical team, we also uncovered a network of these facilities, spread across the entire NAA. Not one has less than three captive women, and the children are being funneled off into so-called "adoption" programs. What we need is hard evidence that can be used to bring them down. We were unprepared last time for what we would find, and rather than risk harm to the women and children, we opted to leave and regroup. Now that we know, we call upon the Resistance to help us breach the local facility, get video footage, and safely wake and rescue the women inside the facility."

My eyes sting at the memory of Josephine, of Aisha, and all the other women we'd had to leave behind. Not again.

"Yes, yes. That's all well and good." Helena waves a hand, and my anger starts to boil at her dismissal of Atlas's request. "But what the

Resistance needs is not what the Royces need. While your cause is worthy, I want assurances up front that this will benefit my people, not only you four."

Someone at her end of the table hisses through their teeth, but I can't pinpoint who.

"So the women trapped all over the country aren't enough incentive for you? Good Lord, do you have a heart at all, Helena? How can you be so cold when hundreds of women and babies are in the balance?" Without realizing it, while I was speaking I rose from my chair, and leaned forward across the table, palms splayed across the top in defiance. I stare her down, and she's silent.

"Despite your childish outburst, I have my own people to worry about. As someone in line for rulership, you might need to tread more carefully yourself, Sadie. Facts are facts—I can't help anyone else if my own people aren't taken care of. We need security, food, and freedom as much as the women in the facility that you want us to risk our lives for. You four waltz in and get caught, the worst that happens is you're thrown back in your gilded cage and assigned a few more guards than just brother dearest and his crew. If my people are caught, we're prosecuted as traitors to the new crown."

"Enough." Patrick's tone is pure unaffected steel from his seat, whereas my urge to leap across the table and rip her throat out is strong.

"Let's lay it all out on the table, Helena. What do you want in exchange for your cooperation?" Patrick asks, giving nothing away—not even an eyebrow twitch to betray his feelings on the matter.

She clenches her jaw, and leans back in her seat in annoyance. For a moment, they stare each other down, and it feels as if the room is holding its breath.

"I want your promise that when you ascend the throne, you will free the Resistance. I want your promise that you'll ensure my people have access to medical supplies, like any other citizens. I want your promise that we'll be free to live the way we see fit, without these archaic marriage restrictions." She taps her fingernail on the table twice more, before going utterly still. "And I want your *word* that you will pursue this to the end, and that justice will be served on whoever is doing this. If you won't guarantee that, we're out. I won't risk my people for anything less than a guarantee that justice will be served for these women."

Patrick opens his mouth to answer, but Atlas holds up a hand to stop him.

"That's quite a wish list, Helena. You and I have known each other long enough to know that if I give an inch, you'll take ten miles. So, why don't you back that list down a few notches. Need I remind you that the future king of the NAA could make your lives *very* unpleasant if he were inclined to."

Her eyes narrowed, and I held my breath as several of her people around the room stiffened in indignation at the threat. Helena bent first.

"Fine, but only because those women need us more than we need you. Medical supplies, through legal, reliable means; and you better make whoever's done this pay, or you'll answer to us."

Patrick smiles at her, and nods. "That seems more than fair. Your people deserve the same medical care as all of our other citizens, and I can assure you that I'll have no issues pursuing whoever is at the root of this."

Her formerly agitated face drops like a mask, and she suddenly looks like the cat who ate the cream. "Ahh, I was hoping you'd say that, Patrick. Ryker, the document please." She holds out her hand, and he passes it to her in a hurry.

Patrick freezes at my side, as if sensing the same as I do that we've somehow been caught out, without knowing when or how.

Helena holds up the long document before the cylinder, and issues a command. "Scan into evidence, and display."

The cylinder shoots a beam of light over the document, and then goes dark for a moment before flashing on once more, this time loading the image in front of each of us on the tabletop.

Skimming quickly, I try to make sense of what's in front of me. It looks like some sort of building commission, on government letterhead. I'm only about halfway through the document, tripping over a lengthy clause about the classified nature of the research when Patrick's voice rings out, cold as I've ever heard it.

"There's no way this means what you think it does. My father would *never* condone imprisoning those women."

She tsks at him mockingly, "Well, Patrick, I guess you'll find out that it's time for dear King Dad to come off the shiny pedestal you've placed him on. This document was signed seven years ago and condones the construction of nine of the secret facilities. I can't wait to hear him try to talk himself out of this one." I want to slap the smug smile off her face, and I've never even met Patrick's father.

From what he's told me, though, the king is not at all power hungry and hasn't campaigned to become king. The people keep re-electing him, and he accepts out of a sense of duty. He's even been the most supportive with keeping Patrick out of politics, until recently. So *why would he imprison all of those women? It doesn't add up.*

"We'll see, Helena. This doesn't prove anything. I'm going to give him a chance to explain himself and get to the bottom of this."

She shrugs, seemingly unconcerned. "Good luck with that, dearie. I don't know how you think you'll get in touch without getting captured, but by all means . . . Just know, if they scoop you back up, it doesn't negate this deal. You're on camera, and everything has been saved for posterity." She snaps, and the table displays a still of Patrick's angry face moments before.

"I'm sure this has been a lot to take in, so maybe you four should go discuss your options. We'll be here when you're ready to move forward with a rescue attempt."

Condescending witch! Sorry, smug son of a—

"Come on, Sadie." Patrick snaps me from my mental tirade, and I stand grudgingly, but trying not to look it. She might have more information for now, but we've got a secret weapon who can change that. *Glitch.*

SEVEN

HIGH WATER

"Patrick, please sit down," I urge, but he ignores me. Atlas has been gone for nearly half an hour to retrieve Glitch from his bachelor's residence, and Patrick's been pacing a track in the floor ever since. Nell and I have moved past outrage, and into damage-control mode. She presses a warm cup of cocoa into my hands, and I sigh in relief at the familiar, comforting smell.

"I can't—if I'm moving, I'm thinking." He rakes his hand through his hair, which is already a mess. "There's absolutely no way my father would be behind this. Half the people in his office? Maybe. His political competition? Sure. But my dad wouldn't hurt a soul. His main critics for years have said he's not tough enough on foreign policy, and he doesn't press our size advantage over Eurasia or the Australian Collective. So how is it I'm supposed to believe he's willing to enslave his own people, and for a reason we still haven't been able to identify?" He stops talking, makes another lap, turns. "I don't buy it. It's got to be a set up."

"Good God, man. It probably is. But we can't prove it if you can't calm down. Your wife is so stressed, she can't even drink her cocoa, so would you take a chill pill for like five minutes? Please? I'm getting tired just watching you." Nell arches an eyebrow at him in challenge.

He sighs, but stills. Satisfied he's not going to run into a wall for the next sixty seconds, I blow on my mug to cool it, before taking a grateful sip. I instantly regret my decision, and gratitude flees my mind as instead of a world of bliss, it tastes foul, and my stomach twists angrily. *Not now, stomach, there's far too much going on.*

I breathe through my nose, teeth clenched for a moment until it passes, and then set the mug aside. Nell and Patrick don't notice, thankfully, as they're still debating the likelihood of a political setup. *I hate politics.* Guilt strikes me instantly at the thought. I'm supposed to be a leader, a political figurehead, and I hate politics. How is that going to work? Is my entire life going to be either hiding from my responsibilities, or letting Patrick—and the people, for that matter—down because I hate the job?

Unease adds to the churning in my gut, but I'm interrupted by the front door swinging shut with a snap. We all turn as Atlas strides in, followed by Glitch. He trips over the edge of the rug, and stumbles the last foot into the room before righting himself, and pushing his glasses up his nose.

"So, Atlas tells me you've all had a really interesting morning! Guess these Resistance people *are* out for blood, after all. I mean, if you ask me, it always seemed a bit too good to be true—they had to want something. Though, I admit, I mostly felt like they'd be asking for some sort of political favor from Patrick now that he's a bona-fide prince and all. I imagine a lot more people are going to want favors now, so it seemed a logical conclusion. But, phew, trying to take the whole thing down from the top! I guess we know that Helena doesn't pull punches, now. She's something else, right? Did you know she recently added a fifth man to her love-triangle situation? Word on the street is that one of her other four relationships is on shaky footing, so she decided to bring in another fella preemptively. I assume they don't call them love triangles, here. Huh, probably should have spent some time today researching that. Terminology is so key to fitting into a new scene." He pauses to tuck a wayward hair behind his glasses, and seems to finally realize we're all staring at him in silence.

"Sorry, was I rambling again?"

Patrick's lips quirk up infinitesimally at the corners. "Not at all, man. We're glad to see you, too. Grab a seat and let's talk."

We all move to the living room, and Patrick tucks me under his arm on the couch, giving my shoulders a gentle squeeze. I lean my head against his shoulder, and try my best to focus on the important details we need to discuss, rather than how nice it feels to be leaning against him, and how good his shirt smells. He's a slice of comfort in the sea of uncertainty that is our lives.

Glitch swings his messenger bag around, and pulls out a familiar silver device to block sounds, and presses the blue button. Once it's active, he gives a short nod. "Okay, people, what do we need?" He's matter-of-fact now, as he pulls out his trusty tablet, fingers poised to type.

Patrick lets out a gusty sigh. "I know where I'd like to start: with clearing my dad's name. But that's probably not where we should start. What do you think, Atlas?"

He looks compassionate, but he's firm when he says, "I agree—that isn't where we should start. We need to first nail down the evidence and free the closest women we can. Once they are safe, we can raid the facility for any information, document what we've found, and destroy the evidence."

Nell interjects, "Why do we need to destroy the evidence? Isn't the point that we're preserving it, to prove what's been going on? How are we supposed to tackle every other tri-state's location if we do that?"

"This isn't a one-and-done situation. Ultimately, we want to free everyone. However, I'm guessing that whoever is in charge is high enough up that they'd shut down and flush the system before letting themselves get caught. So, they can't know they've been caught until it's done. Then we can go to each and every location, and ensure the safety of all the women trapped."

"By flush the system you mean . . ." I swallow, horrible visions in my mind.

"They may kill them all," he says in a somber tone.

"How are people so awful? I just can't comprehend what would drive someone to do something like this." The ugliness of the entire situation feels like an elephant sitting on my chest.

"I know, Sadie. The important thing is that we stop them, for good," Atlas says, voice hardening again. "Glitch, I assume you've got some ideas on the data-gathering portion of the operation?"

He snorts. "Ideas? Saying I've got ideas is like saying Niagara's got water. You don't worry about the data collection. You get me inside that building in one piece, and you'll have more proof than you know what to do with. I will need a minimum of ninety seconds to gather a full video visual before you can have the doctors begin waking the women. There will be doctors, I assume?"

Patrick answers, "Yes, the Resistance will have to provide medical support. I can't imagine they'll be too happy, given the state of their medical supplies, but perhaps I can pull some strings behind the scenes and get them support sooner. Or, barring that, we could schedule the raid after their supply run."

56

Such a compassionate heart. They're trying to blackmail his father, and he still wants them to have adequate medical care. *This is why he's going to be an excellent king one day—he puts the people's needs first.*

"I hate that plan," Nell announces. "The idea of them strapped to their beds one second longer than we can help ticks me off. Let's do this thing! Let's go storm the doors and get them out of there. All this data gathering—no offense, Glitch—and plotting, and . . . let's go get them!"

"Why can't we have the best of both worlds? Get them out quickly, skirt the supply issue, and use that as a decoy of sorts. Why not do both on the same night?" I ask, and everyone looks thoughtful for a moment.

"It could work," Atlas muses. "I was betting on having the full strength of the Resistance to take out any opposition, but maybe it's smarter to have them act as a diversion nearby, as if they're protecting their supply route. They could adjust to run right past the EIC, and cause a distraction that way."

"Do you think they'll agree to that? It would possibly implicate them," Patrick points out.

"There's only one way to find out," Atlas says succinctly.

The afternoon passes in a blur of plotting, planning, and details. Each of us has a say, and in the end the five of us agree the plan is solid. Exhaustion drags at my limbs by the time I crawl into bed, yet as soon as I close my eyes, they pop back open, and I can't do a thing but lie awake, staring at the ceiling in the darkness. In all the day's changes, there was no chance for Nell to request a pregnancy test. So, I lie here, unknowing, rolling it all around in my head. We're on such precarious footing, with so much going on, it would probably be better if I wasn't pregnant. But somehow, I can't bring myself to wish away a tiny carbon copy of Patrick, as I imagine our kids would be.

His dark hair in a little baby curl, those deep blue eyes set in rounded baby cheeks. A sigh escapes me, and Patrick rolls from his side of the bed, arm tucking around my middle in his sleep. My life has changed so much in the past few months, it's hard to comprehend it all sometimes. Days spent in a sun-soaked pasture on Morgan's broad back feel like a long lost memory that I might never get to experience again. A tear slides slowly down my cheek at the thought, and I squeeze Patrick's arm where it rests on me. He stirs, so I relax my grip.

I am strong enough to make it through this, whatever happens. We'll free the women because somebody has to. We'll make things right with the NLC, even if we have to wait until Patrick's a king, because it's what's right. And I have to believe we will succeed—because if we don't, who will?

Something of my distress must have filtered through Patrick's sleep haze, because in an instant, he's kissing my temple, and brushing another wayward tear from the side of my face with his thumb.

"What's wrong, Sadie?" His voice is soft, a whisper in the still night.

So many words in my head, but not one offers itself up to him. Tongue-tied, I shrug the shoulder he's laying on.

He chuckles softly into my hair, and his breath tickles the spot just under my ear. "It's going to be okay, my love."

I shudder at the reassurance, unable to hold it back. *What if it's not okay? What if it all goes wrong?* But I don't say that, I pile it under a mountain of denial in my mind instead. "I know it will, Patrick. Go back to sleep. I'm fine." I pat his arm in a feeble attempt at reassurance.

He sighs but drifts back off. I stare at the ceiling until the sun comes, but sleep never does.

EIGHT

THE FALLOUT

With nothing left to do but wait, Patrick convinces Bushy-Branch to take Nell and me to retrieve baking supplies so I have something to do to stave off the boredom. We're walking back to our temporary home—bags of pantry staples in hand—when Nell stops mid-street, and darts to the left.

"Hey, come back! Nell, what are you doing!" Ajax shouts, startled by her sudden exit. While he doesn't watch us twenty-four-seven, he's still escorting us to and from meetings, and keeping his distance so it's less obvious to the other residents here that we're essentially under lock and key. The supervision rankles, but apparently that's my lot in life these days. No matter how many places I'm shuffled to, *somebody* wants to control my every move.

We all stop in the street, and watch as she disappears through a swinging glass door. Looking up, I see that it's a pharmacy. Five minutes later, she returns empty handed and with a scowl on her face. Ajax shakes his head, and continues escorting us home without comment. Once we're walking again, she grabs my arm and slows me down so we have some space from the rest of the group.

"No pregnancy tests available. The pharmacist very snidely informed me that they don't throw away testing supplies like the NLC—apparently tests are done by blood draw only, and only after ten weeks with no cycle, to 'preserve medical resources.'" She makes air quotes with her fingers.

"Well, I guess we'll just have to wait and see, huh?" I keep my tone light, but my stomach is in knots. Not knowing feels like the sword of Damocles hovering over me. If I am, and people find out, the kidnapping attempts could double. If I'm not, we're back to the drawing board, depending on how things end up with the NLC and the NAA rules. No baby in the next two and a half years, no more marriage to Patrick.

"I know, but it's annoying. It's not like we had much choice in the matter, but he acted like I was some sort of spoiled brat. Me, can you imagine?" She grips her chest dramatically, and I can't help the smile that crosses my face.

"Never! You?!" I slip my arm around her waist, and give her a short but tight squeeze to convey my thanks. "You're the best, Nell. Seriously. I would be going nuts without you here through all this. But, I'm also sorry you got dragged into it." I look down at the pavement—at my boots, so out of place covered in dust in this city.

She scoffs. "Girl, I wouldn't miss this for the world. I've fallen butt-first into a ringside seat to the next phase of humanity as we know it, which is way more excitement than I expected when I snuck out of my uncle's house at three a.m. to hitch a shuttle to the NLC. I mean—you're going to change things. You and Patrick are really, really going to shake things up. Can't you imagine it? You with your perfect genes, him with his perfect hair—your babies will be unstoppable forces of nature." She shakes her fist at the sky to punctuate her point, and a strangled laugh escapes me as we approach our front door.

"Have a nice afternoon, folks. And remember, *low profile*." Ajax glares at Nell as we file past him into the house.

She blows him a kiss and bats her eyelashes as she walks by into the dim entryway.

I shake my head and walk in behind her. *I'll never be bored with Nell around, that's for dang sure.*

Most of the next day and a half are filled with me baking up anything and everything that sounds good. A lot of it I can't stomach, but sweet, sugar-rolled ginger cookies make me feel human again, and I may not eat anything else for the rest of my life. A fresh tray is lying on the counter, with only two minutes left on the cooling timer, when there's a knock at the front door. Since the kitchen is closest to the door, I shuck off my oven mitts, but don't bother removing my apron to talk to the guards. They're probably coming to ask if I've got any cookies ready yet.

They may not be sure if they like us yet, but they *are* sold on my baking abilities. I swing the door wide, and freeze at the sight of a petite brunette, freckles dusted across her nose. "Uhm, hello."

"Hi, I'm your neighbor across the street. It seemed like time we met, since you've had a bit of time to settle in. May we come in?"

My eyes drop down, and I see two identical brown heads peeking from behind her shyly. When they realize they've been spotted, they disappear back behind her.

With a chuckle at their antics, I hold the door wide. "Come on in, uh . . . ?"

"Halle, thank you. And this is Daniel, and Delia."

"Well, it's nice to meet all of you. I'm Sadie. I just pulled some cookies out of the oven—would you like some?" I switch into hostess mode seamlessly, falling back on years of southern hospitality.

"Oh, that would be great, if you have enough to spare?" she questions, and I file that away for later. *How bad is the supply situation here?*

"Of course, we have plenty. And I'll grab Nell, too. She'll be excited to meet you all."

Her eyebrows raise in surprise. "I didn't know there were two women in your family. What does that make you, a quint, or . . ."

I smile, and save her from further guessing. "A quad, for now. It's Nell, Atlas, Patrick, and myself."

"Oh, I see. You're new here, so that will likely change over time."

I ponder her observation as I go knock on Nell's bedroom door. Music thumps underneath, in typical Nell fashion, but I hear her holler anyways. "Coming!" After a moment, the music cuts off, and she opens the door, a bit breathless. "What's up, buttercup?"

I snort a laugh. "We have guests."

She sighs wearily. "Ugh, who is it now? Helena? One of her many man-loves? Or Pierce to recruit you to be in their *grouple* and make genetically superior babies with him?"

"Would you hush? It's real, normal visitors. The woman from across the street, and her kids."

She drops her hairbrush and cheers up instantly. "Well, that's way better. Let's go!" She breezes past me to meet them, and I head to the kitchen to grab some cookies and plates. Nell's voice carries from the other room. "Oh! You're Halle from the street, and hey, soccer superstars! Nice coaching work the other day."

Halle looks confused as I carry in the goodies. "Uhm, what?"

I elbow Nell in the ribs, and she has the good grace to look embarrassed for blurting it out. "Sorry, it's just that we actually saw you in the street, with one of your husbands, err, boyfriends? I'm not really clear on how the titles work yet, but it seemed like you two weren't having a good day. We also saw these two giving a little guy a soccer lesson."

The kids both giggle, and happily accept a cookie. Their mom's face heats, and I want to smack Nell for her comment all over again. "Oh, how embarrassing. Yes, that's me, and sounds just like the twins." She tucks a short, silky strand of hair behind her ear, and stares out the window. "Well, I guess the good first impression is out the window now, huh?"

Twins, that's amazing! I've never met a set outside of my family.

Nell laughs at her blunt assessment. "How about we call it even?"

Halle smiles in response, and it seems we're back on solid footing. "So, it must be complicated having more than one man. How many hub-sicles do you have, exactly? And twins are super rare, so one of them must be a great match." Nell bites a cookie enthusiastically.

"Nell, seriously?" I look pointedly at the kids. She shrugs unapologetically in response, and continues waiting for Halle to answer.

"You guys are *really* new here, huh? I guess I'll give you the lowdown. I have"—she pauses, and clears her throat—"well, *had,* two partners. Tate, who you saw with me in the street, and Danny."

My eyes flit back to the kids, who are completely ignoring us and playing some sort of handheld games. I shovel another cookie on each plate, and little hands immediately grab them without looking up. That brings a small smile, because kids are kids, no matter where they are—and that's definitely something my nephews would do.

"We call anyone in the relationship a partner, to keep it simple," she adds, immediately switching from the painful topic.

"Partner, got it," Nell affirms.

"Yes. So, Danny was my sweetheart. We grew up together in the same tiny town, and always knew we were destined for each other. His parents, however, insisted that we undergo genetic tests to ensure we were a match. The New Life Program was well underway by then, but still optional. So, we did the testing, so confident. We were a very low match, only about twenty percent." She pauses, and looks off to the side, struggling with the raw memory. Clears her throat. "Anyways, after the results, both of our families insisted that we enroll in the program. Danny and I didn't care, we wanted to be together regardless if we ever had kids. Young love, right?"

I give her a gentle smile, and she continues. My heart is breaking at her sincere words, since I already know that this isn't going to end well.

"Anyways, we refused, but they kept after us. After a while, the constant pressure was too much. We were both only children, so the hopes of four parents being dashed simultaneously was a lot, and we were so young." She strokes one of the twin's heads. "We decided to run away together—really live the romantic dream." At that, Halle laughs. "We learned quickly how hard it was with no family support, no money, no way for me to get a job without a baby already in tow. Because for quite some time, there was no baby in tow. Eventually, we heard rumors about a place that would accept you, give you a job, and let you live as you wanted, free of expectation. We got here as fast as we could, and never looked back. Tate came along within a year, and my babies not long after."

"Wow, so the whole multiple-men thing really worked for you."

She quirked an eyebrow. "I assume you think it will work for you, too, or else you wouldn't be here?"

Nell shrugged, and cast a glance my way.

"We're not that far off from your own experience, honestly. Our previous situation wasn't safe. We wanted to be together, without the expectations, and we heard it was possible here. *Different*, but possible. For now, it's only the four of us." I left it at that, as I had no desire to lie to her, after she'd shared with us.

She nodded. "Believe it or not, a lot of couples end up here that way. They want to be with the person they choose, and things change over time as they're ready for a baby." Her hand drops to her belly. "I can't believe I'm about to do this again, without Danny."

My heart twists in misery at her grief.

"He was killed a few months ago, on a mission. We didn't even get his body back to have a real funeral, just a ceremony." Her voice turns bitter, and I can't blame her. The idea of no more Patrick to hold, no closure, no nothing, fills me with dread.

"So, you're expecting again?" Nell asks gently.

"Yes, after six years we thought we were only going to get our two, and were happy with that. This little one was a surprise. I found out right after Danny died. It could be his, you know? It's a long shot, but it could be." She rubs her belly, and I can see the hope written plain as day on her features.

How terrible to finally get to have a baby with the man you loved, but not have him here for it? I struggle to find the words to say which don't sound trite, but nothing comes. "I'm so sorry, Halle. That must feel impossible."

Her responding smile is more of a grimace. "It's impossible and unavoidable at the same time. I don't have a choice except to put one foot in front of the other, and do my best for the kids."

"Will you four be joining us at the gathering this evening? It's informal, but a tradition around here. We all share a meal about once a month if the weather's nice, and usually there's news. Everyone takes the night off to just be together. It's always a good time, and I know a lot of people would like to meet you all."

"Oh, that's so sweet of you! I'll have to check with Patrick and Atlas, but—"

"We won't let them say no!" Nell cuts me off before I can politely turn down the request. I smile politely, despite the worry gnawing at my gut.

"Great, you can walk over with me. If you bring these cookies, you'll be the talk of the town by night's end," she muses, nibbling on the barely-touched cookie.

"Well, we'll have to make more, then!" Nell says with enthusiasm.

Oh, boy. We are going to be in trouble with the guys.

Halle gathers up her kids, I gather up another half-dozen cookies for them to have later, and Nell sees them out.

Nell follows me to the kitchen where I slip my apron back over my head before turning on her. "Nell, what were you thinking? There's no way Atlas is going to agree to this gathering, and I'm pretty sure Helena's guards won't appreciate it, either. Not to mention, we could be recognized! Our cover is ninety percent staying out of sight, not parading in front of the entire population."

Nell shakes her head at me but doesn't look the least bit apologetic. "Sadie, simmer down. You aren't thinking this through."

I reel back in shock. "*I'm* not thinking it through? Really? Do explain."

She props her hip against the counter before answering. "Listen, you're a rule follower, and I get that. Plus, you're also basically the sweetest person in existence, and I love you for that. But we have to know these people, to understand them. And they are more than just Helena and her merry band of meatheads. You're telling me you don't see them differently now, after hearing Halle's story?"

"Of course I do," I agree softly.

"Exactly. They're not just a bunch of weirdo sex fiends. They've run from society for freedom. They don't have the resources we had at the NLC, and how can we judge them? We can't. We need to understand them."

I'm genuinely surprised by her wisdom in this moment, and I stay silent for a while as I ponder. "Okay, I admit you may not be wrong."

She snorts at me. "*May* not be wrong, Mrs. Politician? I'm not wrong. And, my gut tells me we need to go to this gathering. She said they share news, and we haven't heard a peep about anything since we've been here."

My stomach flip-flops at the possibility of finding out what happened after we left. Atlas has been like a dog with a bone pestering the guards, but they've remained tight-lipped about any fallout from our kidnapping-turned-escape.

"We're still going to have to convince the guys," I acquiesce, and turn to the fridge for more butter. "And bake a lot more cookies."

Six hours later, I'm dressed in a clean black uniform, and I've swapped my favorite boots for a pair of ubiquitous black sneakers.

Atlas and Nell had a fight the size of Saskerta about the plan for this evening, but in the end, Patrick sided with us, and that was that.

Rather than deal with our ever-near guards, we all agreed it would be best to go with the element of surprise, and bet that they wouldn't make a scene to retrieve us.

After popping in my green contacts, I pull my hair into a scruffy bun, making sure the bleached section is prominently displayed. It is a tiny detail, but we are trying to hide in plain sight so I opt for something uncharacteristic. Satisfied that I look neat—if not myself—I leave our room to find Patrick and Atlas waiting. Banging pans sound from the kitchen—alerting me to Nell's location—so I walk in to help her gather up the baked goods we are bringing. Cookies being so small, I decided to also make some larger trays of brownies studded with chunks of dark chocolate, and a gooseberry pie.

Goodies in hand, we set out to meet Halle, Tate, and the kids. I immediately spot Branch, my least favorite of our guards, leaning across the street, looking bored. He's messing around with his watch, and doesn't immediately notice us as we make our way across the street to Halle's house. Patrick's knock on the door draws his attention, and his bushy brows mash together in confusion. Before he moves to confront us, the door flings open with a bang.

"Moooo-om, the cookie lady, and her nosy friend, and two stranger-men are here!" Halle's son Daniel calls out unapologetically over his shoulder. "Did you make more of those cookies? Ours are already gone."

Patrick chuckles at his undisguised enthusiasm.

"I did, but you'll have to wait until after supper." Reaching forward, I tap him on the nose.

He sighs. "Why do all moms say that . . ." Turning on his heel, he disappears into the house without further comment, right as Halle bustles toward us.

"Hey, everyone. I'm"—she shakes her head—"I'm *really* sorry about that. Teaching manners to a seven-year-old is like trying to teach a cat to ride a unicycle. They have no interest, and they resent you for trying."

Nell snorts, "I think we're going to be really good friends. Best friends, even. Sorry, Sadie."

I roll my eyes at her antics. "Yeah, yeah. I know how to share. Six brothers, remember?" The statement slips out in the teasing moment, and I freeze, my eyes darting to meet Patrick's. *Stupid, stupid, stupid! How could I let that detail slip?*

Halle's eyes widen, and her partner Tate appears over her shoulder, twins in tow. "Did you say you have *six* brothers?" he asks, by way of introduction.

I chuckle, and I can hear my nerves in the sound. "Oh, yep. That's me, super weird big family girl." I shrug, aiming for nonchalance.

"Wow, that's amazing." He sticks out his hand to shake. "I'm Tate, nice to meet you all." As we all shake his hand in turn, the kids start clamoring for snacks, and the subject is dropped, thankfully. Sending up silent thanks for mercy, we walk down the road in a companionable throng. I cast a quick glance over my shoulder, and see that Branch has given up on casual indifference, and is nearly shouting into his comm watch.

I can't contain my smirk as I turn back around, and Halle spots it. "What's so funny?"

"Oh, nothing. That guy back there has eyebrows that remind me of those fuzzy dotted caterpillars."

She chuckles. "All right, then."

The rest of the walk is uneventful, and we arrive at a large hillside with blankets and picnic tables haphazardly placed all over it.

"Crap on a cracker, I didn't think about a blanket to sit on," Nell grumbles, but Tate waves her off.

"No biggie, we have a picnic table we always claim."

They lead us pell-mell across the hill, to a random table. The nip in the air is stronger here, and I can faintly smell the ocean salt on the continuous breeze.

We set out all of our foodstuffs down the center of a long table, and other groups do the same all around us. Delicious scents reach my nose, as well as the occasional rank waft of a fish dish floating in a greenish sauce.

A man I don't recognize eventually whistles, and the exuberant chatter stops. "Welcome, family. Are we ready to eat?"

A cheer goes up from the hungry crowd, and in the blink of an eye a line has formed, and we're heading towards the back. We spot Glitch at one point, mingling with a group of men. Many other adults stop and introduce themselves to us on their way by our section of the line, and I lose track of all the names and faces before we reach the food. Despite the fun, worry niggles at the back of my mind incessantly.

Nonetheless, the parts of the meal I can stomach are delicious, and I spend plenty of time pushing the rest around my plate when nausea rises up.

While we eat, someone sets out a large flat rectangle. A massive screen slowly unfurls from it, and starts to play a newsreel.

The first clip—Helena giving mundane updates about holiday guard schedules—passes quickly. Next are more unknown faces, and I quickly tune the news out and focus on the antics at our table. I'm nearly crying with laughter as Delia hangs spaghetti noodles from her brother's upper lip, when a voice I'd recognize anywhere pours from the screen.

"We don't know who you are. We don't know where you are. But I promise that we will find you. If you hurt a single hair on their heads, the wrath of the entire NAA will decimate you." Relief floods me, and I have to hold back an ecstatic sob despite his battered appearance. His cheek has a blooming bruise across it, and I can see large purplish smudges all around his neck beginning to turn green at the edges, and the top of a sling on his left arm is in the shot. "We will not rest, we will not stop, and we will not accept any less than the return of both heirs in perfect health. The king has authorized capital punishment on sight for anyone who interferes with the return of the prince and princess, and we will not hesitate to execute his orders on this matter."

I feel like I can't breathe, as I look into Peter's larger-than-life eyes, hardened with resolve. My heart doesn't want to beat, and numb gratitude that he's alive—beaten badly, but alive—is all I can feel. Patrick slips his arm around my shoulders, and presses a kiss to my temple.

"Keep it together, Sadie. He's okay." His words are a bare whisper against my ear.

Swallowing hard, I force a neutral expression back on my face as Candy Thomas from NAA One appears on the screen next to Peter, concern etched across her features as she lays a palm on his shoulder.

"Peter, I can only imagine how hard this must be for you, on a personal level. I myself have no siblings, but Princess Sadie is your younger sister, is she not?"

His voice drops nearly a full octave when he answers, "Yes, she is."

"Do you have a personal message you'd like to share, in addition to the official message from the king's office? If Sadie is out there listening right now, what would you want her to hear from her big brother?"

His eyes tighten at the corners, but he gives no other sign of emotion away. He clears his throat, "We love you, Sadie, and we are coming for you. I'll always come through for you, no matter what."

My heart is in my throat at his message, and I turn away from the screen as Candy continues talking on her own, Peter no longer in the frame.

"It's so sad, honestly," Tate observes. "That poor girl had no clue what she was getting herself into, and she's probably getting butchered in a lab right now." He bites a hunk out of a chicken wing, and chews thoughtfully.

"Tate, how morbid! They're probably holding onto her until they can negotiate something with the royals. Don't you four agree?" Halle's gaze lands on me, and I can see the question in her eyes. *She suspects something.*

"She's far too valuable as the prince's match, I'm sure they'll be surrendered eventually." Atlas's tone is calm and bored, as if he's discussing a squirrel finding a nut under a tree.

Tate shrugs. "Depends on who's got 'em, right? Those crazy butcher cabals wouldn't take the risk of hanging onto them."

"True enough," Atlas agrees, and on that depressing note, everyone lets the subject drop. But Peter's message echoes through my mind.

NINE

IMPENDING

Waiting *sucks*. Honestly, the kitchen sink is drippy, this house is too orange, the decorative obsession with pointy plants is asinine, and if the Resistance leadership don't make up their minds and give us the go today, I'm going to lose my mind. I kick the ground harder, forcing the back porch swing to jerk in time to my mental tirade. I wrap my arms around my other knee, as I mope alone in the dead heat of the day. A single bird flies overhead, and I track its flight with my eyes.

For the thousandth time in the last two days, since the gathering, I replay Peter's message over and over in my brain. His face, his words. The fact that it's a good sign he still seems to have his job after losing us, the worry my parents must be feeling, and how angry it all makes me that I'm still stuck under somebody else's thumb, despite being in the supposed freest place on the entire continent.

My foot slips with the next angry jab at the ground, and a puff of dust rises lazily into the air, making me sneeze. The sliding glass door opens slowly, and Patrick peeks his head out warily. *Smart man.*

"Are you up for some company?" he asks before coming any further.

With I sigh, I nod. "Yes, I'm just being childish. I'll recover."

He chuckles at my admission, and shuts the door behind him softly on his way out, taking the seat next to me on the swing. His arm settles around my shoulders, and I lean into him a little. "That's okay, we're all childish at times. But why don't you tell me what's bothering you today, instead?"

"Waiting. It's the absolute worst. Zero out of ten—do not recommend." I scrunch up my face in annoyance, and he chuckles again.

"Fair enough. I think we'll hear today, though. They're cutting it close as it is."

I blow out a frustrated breath. "Good. They've taken their sweet time, knowing we're stuck in limbo."

He takes over pushing the swing, and we smoothly glide forward and back, the rhythm much more soothing than my angry staccato jolts. I feel my tension begin to ease, and lean a smidge further into his side. "If they aren't willing to help us, we'll switch to plan B."

"We have a plan B?"

"We will if they say no. And a plan C, and a plan XYZ, if that's what it takes. Sometimes you just have to be the last dog holding the bone to get things done."

"Listen to you, sounding like a real country boy. My brothers are going to love it." *If we ever make it home again.*

The thought has tension knotting up my shoulders again, and Patrick reaches up a hand to knead one shoulder gently.

"You've got magic hands. If this whole royalty thing doesn't pan out, we'll get you a job as a masseuse. Women would line up for miles to let you rub them."

He shakes his head. "I didn't think you would be so eager to let me rub anybody but you. You'd better keep those thoughts to yourself around here. We don't want any suitors lining up at the door for either of us."

"Amen."

We swing in amiable silence for a while. When the sliding glass door opens again, it's Atlas who steps out, all business. "They made a decision. We're on for tomorrow night. They approved the two of us, Glitch, Ajax, and two doctors to be the incursion team. They also sent some gear, if you want to come check it out."

"Hold up, what do you mean the two of you and Glitch? What about me and Nell?"

Atlas looks surprised. "You don't have any military or combat training. It seems a pretty logical choice to let you stay here where it's safe."

"Right, because I've *never* felt safer than with Branch looming right outside the door all hours of the night."

Nell hollers over his shoulder, "She has a point—man is not trustworthy. Major creeper vibes. I mean, that mustache . . ."

Atlas rolls his eyes to the heavens before looking at Patrick for backup. None is forthcoming, "You married her, don't look at me to save you now."

"That's just cold, Patrick. We men are supposed to stick together."

Patrick grins from ear to ear but doesn't say another word in defense.

"Are you saying you actually want the two of them to come along? Because I find that hard to believe, given Sadie might be carrying your polymorphic heir right now. You'd be endangering her and the baby if there's an issue with the breech."

Patrick grimaces at the reminder.

I was wrong—*not knowing* is the absolute worst.

"Sadie, what if you and Nell . . ." he starts.

"Don't even finish that sentence, Patrick. We stick together. We started this together, and we're seeing it through. *Together.*"

Nell joins us on the porch, cinnamon roll in hand, frosting on face. "Gee, Sadie, I think I hear a theme there. Do you want to go somewhere together? I'm not sure."

Atlas remains unmoved. "I get it, you want to help. We want you safe, and out of harm's way. If something happens and we're caught, at least you two are still free, and can make alternate plans."

"Uh, beg to differ. If you think Helena is going to let us waltz out of here past her merry band of meatheads without you, you're dead wrong. We'll have traded one cage for another, and this time without the two of you. And for better or worse, I'm pretty fond of you both." I pause, thinking it over before giving Atlas my most menacing squint. "But if you keep trying to leave us here, I might change my mind about that." He doesn't quake in fear, much to my disappointment.

"Patrick—all jokes aside—surely you see the wisdom in them staying here," Atlas presses, tattooed biceps popping under his shirt in his annoyance.

He looks at me, really looks at me. "Sadie, you know there's a risk to both you and the baby if you come along, right? We don't know how many guards will stay behind, or what kind of firepower they'll have. They could be on high alert after we tampered with the facility in Mairmont, and we won't know how effective the Resistance diversion was until we get there."

"I know."

"And you still want to do it, anyways? Both of you?" he asks, including Nell in the decision.

She nods, and I hesitate before nodding as well.

He turns back to Atlas. "Tell them we're all five going, or none of us are going."

Atlas throws his hands up in exasperation. "What are you three thinking?"

"If they don't feel safer here than with us, I'm not forcing them to stay behind. If we lock Sadie up because she *might* be pregnant, we're no better than the rest of the people we're fighting against. She and Nell are adults, they can weigh the risks as well as we can." His voice is firm, brooking no argument.

Atlas shakes his head but doesn't argue further. He glares at Nell for a moment, and then turns on his heel and strides back into the house. Nell looks unfazed, licking cream cheese frosting off her fingers.

"You're in trouble, girl. You better go talk to him." I point after Atlas, but she holds up a finger. The front door slams.

"I'll wait until he comes back." She heads back inside, and we're once again alone on the swing.

"You're really okay with me coming along?" I turn to face him fully, needing to study his expression.

He drops his arm from the back of the swing, and takes my hands in his, swiping his thumbs back and forth a few times before answering. "No, I'm not. But I'm not any more okay with you feeling unsafe staying behind. If I thought there was a guarantee that you'd be safe somewhere, I'd beg you to stay there. But the unfortunate reality of our situation is that we're not surrounded by friends, so we have to decide. For what it's worth, I'll feel better keeping you by my side than apart, no matter where this life takes us." He gives my hands a squeeze, before reaching up and sweeping a strand of hair off my neck and tucking it behind my ear. A shiver steals through me, like it does any time he's touching me.

"Is life ever going to get less complicated?" I ask, tracing his now-familiar face with my eyes, drinking him in. Straight nose, eyes deep enough to drown in, and high cheekbones. His tan has faded a touch since we met, but he's still my bronzed god.

One side of his mouth lifts in a wry grin. "Probably not, if we're honest. Probably not."

"Why do you have to be so practical? Can't you lie, and tell me what I want to hear some of the time?"

Rather than answer, he leans in for a surprise kiss, making my pulse pound in my veins the instant our lips meet. Tipping my head back for better access, I melt into him like butter on a hot skillet. The sizzle between us is just the same, and I hope it never changes.

It turns out, checking tactical gear for three hours straight is incredibly boring. Atlas decides to punish us for disagreeing with him by boring us to death, so we can't actually go on the op with them. I tried to sneak off twice to the kitchen, but both times he called me on it.

Nell managed to fall asleep on the couch despite his incessant prodding, so he finally calls it a night. He stands from his spot at the end of the couch, and ever so gently leans down, and slides both arms under his sleeping wife. He lifts her to his chest as if she weighs nothing, and her head lolls against his shoulder, completely at peace. He starts towards their bedroom, but stops and turns back for a moment.

"Sadie, there's a package for you on the counter. Nell told Halle she needed a pregnancy test, and she had one stashed somewhere. Traded her the last of your cinnamon rolls for it. It should have directions in the bag, but you're supposed to do it first thing in the morning. Try to sleep as late as you can, though. We've got a late night tomorrow." Without another word, he turns and carries his sleeping wife to their bed.

The soft click of their bedroom door may as well have been the shot from a starting pistol. *I'm not going to sleep a wink tonight.*

TEN

OXYGEN

Ugh, *why does the inside of my mouth taste so awful? Metal. It tastes like metal. It's disgusting, is what it is.* The thought is the first thing that hits me the next morning. The second, my urgent need to use the bathroom. With a groan and a lurch, I force myself upright. Taking a moment for my stomach to settle, I then shuffle as quickly as I can towards the bathroom across the cold tile floors.

Patrick is already up and about, but I shut the bathroom door quietly, regardless. Even though I know Nell and Atlas are at the other end of the house, it still feels as if being too loud this early is rude, somehow. Turning, a knot forms in the pit of my stomach as I see the pregnancy test kit waiting on the back of the toilet. My urgent need to pee fizzles away as I stare at it, and I can feel my palms start to sweat, despite the cold.

I take a deep breath, then another. A feeling is racing around inside my chest that I truly can't identify. Am I hopeful? Full of dread? *Do I want it to be positive, or negative?* The thought strikes me, and it feels like an important question to get right—before I take the test—even in this rare moment of solitude.

There's no denying life would be easier right now, with all we have to do, if it were negative. We could carry on with our plans to change the institution, free the captive women, and heck, get to know each other a bit more before bringing another child into this world. *Hopefully.* I amend, because even in my own head, I'm well aware that a positive test doesn't guarantee that all will be well.

I let out a gusty breath, my chest tight with nerves. I'm not throwing up right now, which could very well mean I ate something bad, and had a stomach bug the last few days. I could be on the mend right now, and this was all a big hubbub about nothing. For some reason, that thought doesn't lighten my mood in the slightest.

There's your answer, Sadie.

No longer able to put it off unless I want to leave a puddle on the floor like an excitable puppy, I stop thinking about it and do the test. A few drips from a disposable dropper into the test receptacle, close it up, shake, and then all the little dots along the test will color according to the strength or absence of the HCG. According to the instructions Nell relayed, it only takes thirty seconds to read, so by the time I've washed up, it's ready.

I can't bear to look. It's the most juvenile thing that I may have ever done, but without looking at it I clasp it in my palm, facing down. I give myself one last look of terror in the bathroom mirror, and then go out to find someone else to tell me if I'm pregnant or not. I poke my head out of our room, and find the living area empty.

The telltale sounds and smells of coffee from the kitchen lead me there first. However, instead of Patrick, I find a bed-headed Atlas with a cup of coffee and a rumpled white t-shirt which I can see his tattoos through. Even freshly rolled out of bed, I still find him intimidating for some reason. He takes me in, and his eyes quickly land on my clenched fist.

"Is that what I think it is?" he asks, voice unruffled, as always.

My throat is tight, so I nod rather than give away my nerves.

"What's the verdict?" He raises one eyebrow in question, and I quickly shrug one shoulder. Just a quick, jerky up and down. That's all I can do. *I can't look. I'm going to puke.* No, *faint.* No, *definitely puke.*

My expression must say it all because he seems to grasp my dilemma. He sets down the cup of coffee, and his expression softens. "Ahh, I see. Would you like me to look?"

His gentle tone takes me by surprise, and I remain frozen in indecision for a single moment before I jab my hand out at him. He takes the test from me, but surprises me when he doesn't look immediately. Instead, he walks around to a bar stool at the counter and pulls it out for me. I gratefully sit down on the pineapple-covered seat, and bite my lip as I stare expectantly at him.

"One minute," he says, and walks to the sliding glass door to the back yard. The door scrapes along the track, and he calls Patrick.

He must have been exercising in the backyard. I should have thought to check there. This is so far from Atlas's job. What is wrong with me? I'm about to stand when a familiar arm slides around my shoulders, and all the tension drains out of me with that single touch.

Patrick.

Atlas stands across the bar in front of us, cool and collected, but with an understanding smile. "Ready?" He looks at me, and then Patrick. I nod, and hold my breath. Patrick must have done something similar, because he finally looks down and opens his palm to read the test.

For a long moment, the silence hangs in the air like the first frost of the season, bitter cold and unexpected. But when he looks up, a smile is plastered on his usually stoic face. "Congratulations, guys. You're parents."

My heart stutters in my chest, and before I can process my own feelings at the announcement, I look over at Patrick, where the biggest grin I've ever seen is spreading across his face. "Really? It's positive?" He sounds incredulous, even though we'd suspected.

Atlas walks over and sets the little egg-shaped device in front of us, and there they are, little pink test bubbles showing how far along it estimates I am. He claps Patrick on the shoulder, and then gives my shoulder a gentle squeeze before he leaves the room.

Patrick turns to me the instant their bedroom door clicks shut, and wraps me in a bear hug. For a moment—just one—everything is right in the world. It's like everything clicks into place, and all the mess and struggle and chaos that's led us here to this moment was worth it. Because truly, there is no other man on the planet I'd rather be sharing this moment with. And my heart blossoms with joy in my chest.

A long sigh escapes Patrick and ruffles my wild morning hair. "What is it?" I ask, the first words I've spoken all morning. Now that we know, it feels like I can breathe again.

He leans back and cups my cheek, and the look on his face is pure adoration. His thumb trails gently along my cheekbone, and his words take my breath away all over again. "I get to keep you. We're having a baby, and now there is no reason for anyone to try to separate us, ever again. No mandatory divorce. No other forced matches, no matter what happens tonight. Me and you, until death do us part. I'm so, so relieved." His voice cracks on the last word, and tears of gratitude clog my throat anew.

This time it's me who pulls him into a crushing embrace, and I might never let him go again. Because I don't have to, and I won't have to. I get to keep him, too.

ELEVEN

GO TIME

Adrenaline is coursing through my veins, and flickers of doubt run through my mind at lightning speed. I push them aside and—for the third time since we've been riding in the back of this truck—check my shoelaces. Still tied. A wheel hits a pothole in the road, and my teeth clack together so hard they hurt.

"I heard that from here," Nell observes, cool as a cucumber from the other side of the transport vehicle.

I rub my jaw absently. "Thanks for the commentary. How are you not nervous right now?"

She glances to her right, where Atlas looms, menacing, in all black, with knives strapped all over him, two pistols in a chest harness, and a rifle barrel poking over one shoulder. "MM won't let anything happen to me, so why be nervous?" She leans over to an un-weaponized spot, and plants a kiss on his arm.

"MM?"

"Muscle Mountain. It's his favorite nickname."

"It is *not* my favorite nickname," he grouses, and looks out the front window.

"Which makes it *my* favorite nickname." She gives me a Cheshire grin, and I can't help but shake my head at their antics. They are a weird pair, but they are oddly perfect for each other.

I glance at Patrick, but he's leaning back against the wall of the transport, eyes closed, and ignoring our conversation.

My hand absently drops to my side, feeling the overlapping scales of the body armor underneath my shirt. It's light, but still uncomfortable where it presses into my side if I slouch at all. It's digging into the tops of my thighs, but I won't complain about the extra protection.

Finally, the truck rolls to a stop a few feet away from our transport helicopter, parked at the end of a long, grassy field.

When the motion stops, Patrick's eyes pop open, instantly alert.

"Everybody out—Mav's waiting and she gets pissy when she's waiting long," the driver says over his shoulder.

Her familiar figure stands by the wing of the plane, close-cropped black curls, and red leather bomber jacket ready for action. "Took y'all long 'nough. I was 'bout to get bored, here in a minute." She studiously picks beneath one nail with a silver file.

Glitch pushes his glasses up, looking green around the gills. "We appreciate your patience, Mrs."—he belches loudly—"Mrs. Maverick."

"Patience ain't got nothing to do with it, boy. And don't you go puking in my clean 'copter. I ain't mopping up after ya." She levels a frank stare at him, nods at the rest of us, and climbs in without further comment.

"I like her more every time we see her," Nell says lightly as we climb the few steps to board the helicopter.

"Contrary women tend to stick together," Atlas comments drily.

She smacks him on the arm. "I'll remember that later. When I decide to be *extra* contrary."

"Yippee."

"You two cut it out—we all know you actually like each other," I demand.

"Well, duh. You don't pick at people you hate." Nell pecks him on the cheek before taking her seat, and the big old Muscle Mountain smiles at her like she hung the moon.

With no warning, the chopper lurched from the earth, spurring us all to jump into our harnesses.

Rather than two-way headsets, the cabin was wired with speakers, so that we could hear Mav. "Y'all hang on now, y'hear? I ain't takin' all day."

The chopper zips and dips a bit wildly before gaining altitude, and it feels like being strapped to the back of a bumblebee. *Bumbling.* I look over at Patrick, and find him gazing serenely at me already. He reaches over and runs a finger down my jawline ever so slowly, but doesn't say a word over the noisy helicopter blades. I get lost in his gaze for a moment, sharing a secret smile with him before surveying the rest of our group. Nell is swinging her feet freely, like a kid on a roller coaster while she looks with rapt attention out the window. Atlas is staring straight at the ceiling, unflinching, probably reviewing the plan in his mind for the thousandth time since we agreed to it. Glitch has his head as close as he can get to his knees while still wearing the harness, and a bag hovering about an inch below his nose. Ajax sits across from him, keeping a wary eye on Glitch's airsickness. Two doctors, Vance and Courso, and their nurse, Winston, fill out the rest of the row with Ajax.

After surveying the other passengers, I slowly shut out my surroundings, and hone in on the plan. Atlas is in charge of the breach, in formation with Ajax and Patrick. He's been drilling them for a few days to get them up to his standards. The medical team are next, followed by Nell and me to assist as the women wake, getting them out the door. Winston has given us a rundown of what we're supposed to monitor for, so we can actually help. And Glitch is the camera whiz, getting the footage we need, and making sure no video of us leaks in the process.

It's a solid plan, with no loose parts or extraneous people. Maverick will be standing by with the helicopter to air-lift the women and medical staff as soon as they're cleared. The rest of us will destroy the building, and then follow on land.

The helicopter begins to drop, and I reflexively grab my harness straps. Our descent is rapid, and the lights inside our vehicle abruptly shut off, as if we've lost power. "Don' fret now, we're gettin' close. When I give the count, you unbuckle and prepare to roll' out."

Glitch retches, punctuating the order quite effectively. One of the doctors—Courso, I think—reaches into a cargo pocket on his arm and slaps a patch of some kind on the back of Glitch's neck. Glitch starts, but after another minute he sits up and wipes his mouth on the back of his arm.

Mav's voice comes over the speakers this time, low enough that I have to strain my ears to hear it, "Five, four"—I hurriedly unbuckle my chest straps—"three, two"—one last anxious glance at Patrick, whose brows are drawn down with intensity—"one. It's showtime, folks." The helicopter hovers for a split second more before we tap the grass with barely a bump.

Atlas flings the side door open, and leaps to the ground, completely ignoring the two steps into the aircraft. Ajax is right behind him, and Patrick after that. They disappear into the waning night, and the medical team climbs down straight after, taking the stairs. Nell and I grip hands, and make our way down the steps together. Her tight fingers on mine drag me back into that moment hiding in a bathtub in Mairmont, with the sounds of bombs going off in the background as we prayed for safety. I shove the fearful memories aside, and strain my eyes to see in the dim light. We aren't using lights on the way in, until we've cleared all guards. Glitch is hot on our heels, with seemingly no lingering effects from his earlier sickness.

We weave through dense trees and shrubs, following the hushed sounds of the medical team in front of us. They stop after a few hundred feet and drop to their haunches behind some scrub. The three of us pick some shrubbery a few feet to the left and do the same. Through a gap in the branches, I can barely make out the black fatigues of our men as they approach the door. No one stands guard outside—or they've already taken care of them—which seems like a good sign. Atlas reaches forward and sticks something an inch outside the door handle, and then gestures right and left for them to scan the exterior of the building. Glitch is to my right, hand up over the shrubbery scanning with what looks like a night-vision camera. The three men disappear around the edge of the building, and long minutes pass in silence. The watch on my wrist vibrates, and within seconds flames light the sky to the west, and we know our diversion has started in earnest.

The sounds of cranking engines pierce the clearing, and two ATVs with guards on back peel off down a narrow path, so similar to what we used to discover the facility at Mairmont. Before they're out of sight, I hear the cracks of two rifles firing—so closely timed that it might have been one—and the ATVs stop dead in their tracks, riders toppling over. Other than the purr of ATVs and the distant commotion, the clearing is still for three breaths, before Ajax runs out from the back of the building, to check the two guards. After checking them both, he removes the keys from the ATVs, and gives a closed-fist signal to Atlas and Patrick, still tucked away out of sight behind the building.

Even though I know it's coming, the sound of the door grenade detonating still makes me jump sky high. Nell's hands wrap so tightly around my biceps at the noise that it's like she's digging in with sharp talons instead of fingers. The light from the blast fades slowly from our vision as it clears, and the front door of the facility is swinging from a single steel hinge, a hole torn clear through the space where a doorknob used to be, and the bottom half torn off. Atlas rounds the building first, pistol up, and Patrick tight on his shoulder. By the time they reach the door, Ajax has their back for the entry. Atlas clears the hallway with three quick shots from the pistol, and once again they vanish from sight into the building. I hold my breath, unable to think until my watch buzzes again, two short blasts. *It's go time.*

The doctors leap to their feet, and we're dogging their steps as we approach the entrance with the still-dangling door. I duck around the jagged metal edges. After the darkness of the woods, the bright tube lighting and stark white walls burn my retinas like staring into the sun. The building is eerily familiar, and we dart down the first hall to the right, where we found the girls trapped in the last facility. Sure enough, there's a nearly identical room, but this time there are only four women strapped to hospital beds. The

92

rest of the dozen beds in the room lie empty. Winston shucks off a large backpack filled with medical supplies, and the doctors empty their cargo pockets of syringes and drug vials while Glitch does a visual sweep of the room with yet another camera. As instructed, we are standing back so he can scan continuously without us being in the final film. He makes a circuit of the room, capturing each woman's face, and the ID number on her monitor. After the fourth woman, he darts out the door and back up the hallway to continue scanning the entire building. The doctors jump forward like runners off a starting block, and take patients on opposite sides of the room. They quickly assess the drug labels, to ensure they're as anticipated before pushing syringes of medication into the IVed arms of each woman, and moving to the next. Nell and I wait in nervous anticipation, ready for our time to help.

Stethoscope in hand, Dr. Vaughan monitors the woman's pulse until whatever he's expecting happens, and turns to give me the nod. I jog over, and take her cool hand from the bed. The air smells strongly of sterilizer, and the scent burns my overly-sensitive nose. Searching the file at her feet, I see a name there. Ana Linsey. She doesn't have a visible baby bump, so either she's not pregnant or it's very early on. Either way, hopefully she'll have an easier time of recovery. I scan the rest of the faces and bellies in the room, and one seems very large, surely near term. Re-training my eyes on her monitor screen, the numbers gradually move into the ranges Winston told us to expect, and each minute feels like an eternity.

Noise in the hallway draws my attention, but a fluttering movement in my hand drags me straight back. Her thin, narrow fingers try to clutch my hand, and her eyes are huge with panic.

"Ana? Ana, it's okay. My name is Sadie. A lot has happened, but we're here to take you somewhere safe. Can you hear me, Ana?"

93

Her grip on mine is weaker than a baby bird's, but with great effort she's able to nod. Her other hand floats up, and touches her throat with an urgent gesture.

"Water! Yes, Ana, we have water for you. Let's try to get you to sit up first." She gives the barest nod, and her already waxy complexion takes on a sheen of sweat as I find the button and the bed starts to rise.

"Sadie, catch!" Winston calls as he lobs a water pod in my direction. I catch it one-handed, and then have to release Ana's to twist it open. She eyes the small container of water with blatant lust in her eyes, and I carefully help her hold it to her lips. She sucks it down greedily, and splutters painfully.

"Th-ank you," she says in a cracked whisper. "What ha-ppened? Wh—" Her voice gives out.

"I'll explain everything, Ana. But first we've got to get you out of here. Do you think you can stand if I support your shoulders?"

Wary determination fills her thin, pale face, and she shifts to swing one leg over the bed. Her movement is painstakingly slow, and I know we're going to have to move faster if we want to get everyone to safety before our distraction ends. Racking my brain for options, I see that Nell's patient hasn't woken yet, and Winston is also by her side.

I whisper-yell, "Nell, help me! We'll get them out faster if we double up and carry them." Winston nods agreement, and Nell darts to Ana's bedside. As gently as we can, we swing her legs down over the side of the bed, and she grimaces.

"Tingles. Pins, needles."

"I'm sorry, Ana. I wish we could give you more time, but it's unsafe here." I try to keep my voice steady and reassuring.

"I'm tough, let's go." Her hands shake like leaves in a hurricane, but her voice is filled with steel will.

Nell and I scoop her up under each shoulder, and find she's light as a feather when we lift her from the bed.

She lets out a moan, but doesn't say anything as we carry her from the room, and down the hallway towards the hanging door. We've almost reached it when there's a yell from over our shoulders.

"Sadie, wait! Nell!" It's Atlas, at the far end of the hallway. "We've cleared inside, but we don't know how soon guards will be back, so one of us needs to go with you back to the transport."

He jogs around us and scans the clearing before signaling over his shoulder and leading the way across. We move in silence, and a look at Ana's face shows her lips tight in determination to remain silent as well. *She's so brave. She has no idea what's going on, yet she's hanging on for all she's worth.*

We have to slow down when we reach the brush, and Atlas carries a pistol in his right hand, and a wicked-looking black blade in his left. Holding branches out of the way whenever possible, he guides us on the clearest path back to the helicopter. Long minutes later, feeling very winded, the welcome sight of Mav standing outside the door to the helicopter greets us. We pick up the pace again, and Atlas stops to stand guard as we close the final distance.

"I'm going back to help the others, you two stay here. We can buddy up and get the last three out without you." Without waiting for agreement, he disappears back into the tree line, his black-clad frame blending seamlessly with the night.

Nell sighs, "I don't like it one bit."

"Me either," I agree, but all we can do is help Ana into the helicopter, and get her strapped into a seat. It takes us several minutes to position her, buckle her, and get her settled with a blanket, an emergency nutrient-gel pack, and a second water pod as we were instructed. By the time we're done helping Ana, we see Patrick and Doctor Vance carrying the heavily pregnant woman between them, still looking like dead weight on a makeshift stretcher.

"Clear the floor! They haven't been able to wake her yet, so we're going to stabilize her horizontally." Patrick huffs out the directions, and we scramble to comply.

The minutes pass in a blur of frenzied activity, settling woman after woman into the helicopter. Three of the four were able to be woken, and by the time we're done they're all settled into a seat next to a doctor or Nurse Winston, looking very confused and pale. Mav's expression has turned to darker storm clouds with each new woman that's appeared, and by the time we're done loading she's spitting mad, and ready to tear somebody's head off.

"It ain't right, what's been done to these po' women. Rumor is there's more of 'em—that true?"

"It is. Glitch has a list," I confirm, feeling wiped out.

"You tell your Glitch that I'll drive to e'ry one of 'em until we snatch these women out o' there. This ain't right, and Mav ain't 'bout to let no'one stay like this as long as I got wings to carry 'em out o' there. You hea' me? We gon' get every. Last. One." Her cajun accent gets thicker as she gets more riled up, and jabs her finger into the panel of the helicopter, before Doctor Courso calls out that they're ready for takeoff.

"Fly safe, Maverick," I say, stepping back towards the tree line. I look around, and see that once they take off it will only be me and Nell left here, and the hair stands up on the back of my neck. Each of the men on the combat team has returned to the facility to finish their cleanup and destruction job, and we haven't seen hide nor hair of Glitch since he initially swept the room.

Mav climbs into the pilot's seat and turns back to us before shutting the door. "You done real good in there, today. You're good people." She shuts the door with a final snap and, in another breath, the blades start turning, forcing us to take cover lest we get blown over by the downdraft.

Nell and I cling to each other, just inside the tree line as the helicopter lifts higher and higher, blending with the night sky except for the noise of the blades. *Chop-chop-chop-chop* . . . As the sound begins to fade, we both turn our attention to the fires on the western horizon. They seem smaller, which is a sure sign our window of opportunity is about to slam shut. With no sign of our pickup vehicle yet, we decide to walk back towards the facility, so we'll hopefully meet the men halfway.

We're almost back when we hear voices, and freeze. The familiar sound of Patrick's voice causes the tension to drain from my shoulders. We pick up the pace, and have almost reached the edge of the forest when an explosion blinds us as it nearly knocks us off our feet.

TWELVE

REVERBERATE

When the blinding white fades from my vision, my ears are still ringing, and my limbs shaking like leaves. I look over and see Nell holding her ears, looking wild-eyed as well. Reaching over, I grab her by the forearm and lead her forward, so we stay together. But I have to know that Patrick's okay, and he was closer to that explosion than we were.

We stumble forward, dodging trees and scrub brush and finally stumble into the clearing. The men are all there, Patrick, Ajax, and Glitch leaning over Atlas, on the ground. Nell snatches her arm out of my grip and runs to him, dropping to her knees at his side. When I get close enough, I see he's bleeding profusely from a head wound.

"What happened?" I yell.

Patrick turns and squints, and I can tell he still didn't hear me.

"WHAT HAPPENED?" I try again.

"SHRAPNEL. I THINK HE'LL BE OKAY, JUST HAVE TO STOP THE BLEEDING," he hollers back.

I turn back to Atlas, but see Nell's already on top of it. She's pulled gauze and tape from her cargo pants pockets, and is applying firm pressure as Glitch fumbles the tape roll with shaking hands. Patrick takes it from him, and swiftly removes several long pieces and passes them to Nell, who efficiently binds the gauze to his head. Finished, she grabs him under one arm, and Patrick grabs him under the other, and they haul him to his feet. With his legs wobbling like a newborn foal's, I worry they're all going to tumble straight back down so I hurry around and place two hands firmly against his back to steady him.

Once he stops swaying in the breeze, we walk at a painstaking pace towards the clearing's edge. The hike out of the woods is slow, and Patrick trades off supporting Atlas's right side with Glitch, so he can watch our backs until we reach our pickup location. Glitch is leading us based on a pre-programmed GPS coordinate in his comm watch. Or knowing Glitch, some other gizmo he invented.

Thankfully Atlas gets steadier on his feet as we go, and by the end he's able to walk with only Nell for support. We exit the dense brush at an unpaved side road, and I couldn't be happier to see a ubiquitous black vehicle idling there, waiting for us. The back hatch pops open at our approach, and Patrick confirms the driver's ID before we pile into the cargo hatch. Atlas leans wearily against the backrest of the bench seat while Nell checks underneath the bandage.

"The bleeding's stopped, so I think you'll be all right. But we'll need to get you checked out by one of the doctors to make sure. It seems like it only grazed you, so you were really lucky." Her voice wavers at the end, and for the first time in our acquaintance, Nell bursts into tears. Atlas heaves his arm up and around her shoulders, and pulls her into his side. He slowly leans down and plants a kiss on the top of her head.

"It's okay, Nell-bell. I'm okay." He shushes her and holds her, and we all ride in weary silence as our ride bumps over the unpaved road.

Eventually the tires meet pavement, and we pick up speed. Nell's tears have long since dried, and she's sleeping peacefully tucked into Atlas's side. She looks young there. It's easy to forget she's only seventeen when she's awake and full of fire and vinegar.

Glitch pushes his glasses up his nose, and fiddles with the gadget in his hands for the umpteenth time. He finally speaks, "What happened back there? That detonation was way too close to us."

Atlas shakes his head. "I don't know, man. I didn't pull the trigger. It was on a remote switch, set to ignite a fast burn from what we were told, to make it look like equipment malfunctioned, then caught on the oxygen supply in the treatment room."

"Well, either they lied to us, or it was defective. Either way—"

Patrick's look is grave as he finishes the thought—"It's time to call my father."

Eighteen hours later, Atlas has been cleared by the medical team; we've confirmed that three of the four women are awake and confused, but otherwise doing well, all things considered; and we've all crashed. After a lengthy shower in the cactus-themed bathroom in our room, I emerge with my hair wrapped in a towel feeling tired still, but squeaky clean in my standard-issue Resistance black sweats. Patrick's sitting on the edge of our temporary bed, elbows on his knees.

"Hello, Mr. Royce, what brings you here this evening?" I ask in my best flirty tone, and put one hand on my hip.

The smile he flashes me is appreciative, but wan. "Hey, Mrs. Royce. You, of course." His words return my flirty gesture, but his heart isn't in it.

I plop onto the bed next to him, and wiggle my arm around his to rub the inside of his forearm. "What's wrong, Patrick? I expected you to be a lot happier, given we just successfully saved four women and four babies last night."

He sighs. "I am happy about that, truly. But, here we are—still in the middle of a mess—and I don't see a clear way out."

That's my Patrick, always looking ahead to the next hurdle. "Did you get in touch with your dad?"

"No, not yet. That's not how it works, exactly, though. I have a secure phone number for him in case of emergency, where I leave a message with a return number, and he'll call me back when he's in a private location. So, I should hear back in eight to twelve hours. Although, it may be sooner given the presumed kidnapping." He says this all in a bland tone, as if it's the most normal thing in the world to have a secret, memorized phone contact for your politician father across the continent.

Tension coils in my stomach, but I keep my voice calm when I ask, "And we're sure they won't trace anything, and come swoop us up before we've figured this out, right?"

"Right. Glitch has secured a clean phone, and done his voodoo on it to make it untraceable." He points his thumb toward the living room, where Glitch's choppy snores penetrate the thin walls from his spot on the couch. I must have been exhausted after the mission because I didn't notice at all last night.

"So, now we wait."

"Now we wait," he agrees.

"What do we do in the meantime?" I ask, doodling little shapes on the inside of his arm with my fingertips.

He shrugs. "Great question. Rest, try to keep you away from explosions, and review the footage Glitch got last night. Make a plan, again."

It's my turn to sigh. *There's always another plan.*

After we eat some breakfast-turned-dinner, the five of us follow Ajax and Branch back to headquarters, to debrief and share the mission footage with the Resistance leadership. Nell links arms with me, and does her sassiest walk along the way, and everyone chats amiably. We're all in high spirits after a successful mission, despite hitting a few snags along the way.

We arrive at the headquarters, and it's lacking the hustle-and-bustle we saw the first time. Only a few people are lingering inside around a sleek chrome coffee machine, plus we can already see people seated around the long black table in the fishbowl conference room. Wasting no time, we cut straight there, and our chatter dies out as we cross the threshold.

After taking a seat close to the door, I glance around the room and see there are only two empty seats remaining at the other end of the table. We all sit in awkward silence, and it's evident, as usual, that we are not on the same team. No one wants to shoot the breeze, or risk giving away an important detail. Ajax hovers behind us, leaning beside the doorway with a bandage on his hand that I hadn't noticed before. With nothing else to do, I observe each person seated around the table, imagining what brought them here. Once I've exhausted that avenue of thought, I examine the room. It's empty save the table, chairs, the control cylinder, and a potted plant with purple flowers on a stand behind Glitch's seat.

I'm jolted from my woolgathering when Helena and Brock breeze in, at least fifteen minutes late. "Well now, aren't you a lively bunch. Shouldn't you look happier, after such a smashing success?" She doesn't bother to fog the windows this time, since the building has now fully cleared out.

Atlas grumbles under his breath, but I miss whatever it was as I'm watching Brock pull out the head seat for Helena, and slide her back in. His hand lingers on her shoulder a bit longer than strictly proper before he takes his own seat.

She claps red-nailed hands together. "Let's get down to it. Who wants to begin the debriefing?"

Ryker springs to his feet, and starts rattling off the details of the supply run and diversionary portion of the mission. Everyone nods along, and it sounds like they've fully resupplied everything except some seed potato varieties they were hoping to prep for next year so they'd be less reliant on outside food sources.

Next, Doctor Courso stands, and gives a brief statement on the women's health status, and the fact that the fourth woman still isn't responding to their current attempts to wake her. She is starting to have contractions, and they're worried that the stress is interfering with her body's response to the drugs she was held under.

"How long has Paige been held under sedation, doctor?" Helena asks.

He looks grim. "She's been held the longest of these four. As far as the records Glitch was able to provide and what we gleaned from her medical file at the facility, she's been a captive for nearly seven years. She's the oldest, the furthest along in her pregnancy, and she's been bed-bound for so long . . . she may not have the strength reserves needed to recover. But we'll continue doing our best to rouse her, and give her a chance at rehabilitation. They've all got a long road ahead, but her outlook is the most grave."

Seven years. Sweet Jesus, help her.

Helena presses on coolly, undeterred by the awful news. "Did the file say how many children she's birthed in that time?"

"This is her sixth full-term pregnancy."

"No wonder they kept her so long." She taps her nails idly on the tabletop, and the sound feels like it's drilling directly into my skull. "Any mention of the sperm donors for the infants?"

"Not by name, but there was a list of donor's numbers in her file. It's possible someone with the right access might be able to connect those numbers to real men." He glances out of the corner of his eye at Glitch, before focusing in on Helena.

"Good, we'll see if we can make that connection. If she doesn't make it, the baby has a father somewhere." She raps her knuckles twice on the table, and then points at Atlas. "You're up. Show us what you've got for footage."

Before Atlas can move, Glitch starts talking a mile a minute, "Actually, Helena, I'll take it from here, if that's okay? I mean, I assume it's okay, since Atlas isn't the one who took the footage. I mean, he was the one in charge of the rescue mission, which you all already know was executed *quite* successfully. Very impressive, frankly, Atlas's field skills. You should've seen him! The way he just charges in there like—"

"By all means, Glitch, please stand and present your findings." Helena's tone is bone dry, and she gestures for Glitch to stand.

"Oh. Oh, yes, of course!" He slams his chair backwards—right into the potted plant on the decorative wire stand, which tumbles gracelessly to the floor—as he rises. "Oh, look at me! I'm sorry. What a mess. Here, give me a moment, to, to—" he drops to his knees and starts scooping the black potting soil back into the pot with both hands, before righting the now crooked purple flower, and setting it back atop the stand.

Everyone around the table stares in bemused silence at his erratic motions. Before I can get fully out of my seat to help him, he's already back upright.

He stands, drags his hands up and down his pants to knock off the dirt, and then shoves his glasses back up his nose, leaving a big streak of black behind, right up the middle of his nose. "Now, where was I? Oh, yes, the footage." He reaches into his pocket, and pulls out a camera. "So, the initial recording was highly successful. I was able to capture quite a bit of damning evidence, from the exterior of the building with it's clearly disguised setting, continuously throughout a tour of the building, starting with the sedated women, images of their charts with identification, and then more continuous filming down the hall to the security offices, where I scanned as much data as possible with the camera utilizing a hacking program I'd pre-prepared for the purpose of opening and displaying files in rapid succession, all while copying the device for later perusal in depth. Really nifty little piece of code, actually." He pauses to take a breath, and as I look over to Helena, I notice Brock off to her side, jaw muscle twitching in irritation.

He might have been a handsome man, even quite a bit older than I am, if he didn't always have such a mulish expression fixed on his face. His buzz-cut and the streaks of silver in his hair give him that hardened, mysterious look, but at this exact moment he looks like

105

he wants to whack Glitch over the head with one of the conference room chairs.

”As I was saying, all of the footage was continuous, so a professional can verify no edits have been made when presented for evidence, which is key. That, combined with the women's own testimonies and their apparent non-deaths should provide for a *very* open-and-shut case when it's time to present this to, well, whoever we need to present this to.” He grins, quite pleased with himself.

I gesture to my nose, and make a wiping motion. He quirks an eyebrow at me, but doesn't take the hint.

“Thank you, Glitch, so will you be presenting any of this wonderful footage of yours to us, so that we can share in the feat you've accomplished?” Her mocking tone makes me want to slap her, but I resist the urge.

“Oh, no, unfortunately that won't be possible. Maybe not for quite some time, actually.”

Now Helena's jaw has joined Brock's in twitching. *Glitch can be a bit much at times, but these two are going to chip a tooth if they keep clenching their teeth so hard.*

“Well, you see, due to the faulty timing and execution of the final incendiary device, the camera was damaged before we made it away from the scene.”

“Pardon?” She arches a white-blonde eyebrow at him, ire dripping from the single word like poison.

“Apologies. 'Incendiary,' as loosely defined by Webster's twenty-seventh edition, means 'relating to, weaponry such as bombs designed to start fires or incite arson.' Or also 'inflame,' but I don't feel that piece of the definition really applies in this case.” He finally seems to read the rising anger in the room, and rushes to add, “

Uhm, ma'am." He nervously spins the camera around in his hands as he looks back and forth between Brock and Helena, clearly the power couple in this room.

This time it's Brock that slaps his hand on the table and shouts, "Good God, man, we know what incendiary *means*, we gave you the bomb! How can we use the footage if the camera's broken? Did you upload it somewhere?"

"Unfortunately, no."

Brock groans, "How can a so-called technical *genius* such as yourself not have thought to upload the damn footage? The gossips over at NAA One have auto-uploaders, and you want to tell me you don't?"

Glitch reels back as if he's been slapped, and Patrick rises to his feet in defense. "How about we all take a step back, and allow Glitch to finish explaining the situation, before jumping on him? I knew ahead of time that there wouldn't be an upload, due to security. Right, Glitch?"

"Yes, that's right."

"How nice of you to volunteer to explain it to us, then. Succinctly, if you would," Helena says coldly now that she's regained a modicum of composure.

"Well, Glitch is certainly more qualified than I am, but I'll be happy to relay what I can. Auto-uploader technology is owned in its entirety by the Eurasia Alliance. All of the destination servers are leased to the other countries for proprietary uses, but Glitch informed me that it is known they have backdoor access to each server, and there have been major leaks in the past when something of particular political value makes it onto one of their servers. Given that we want to control the spread and audience of this footage tightly, we didn't feel it was worth the risk to back it up remotely, and his equipment for backing it up securely was stored in the pickup vehicle ahead of time for exactly that reason. However, due to the premature detonation of the bomb we were provided, the camera was damaged."

"I fail to see how any of this is good news! We expended an enormous amount of Resistance resources, and you're telling me it was for nothing?" Helena snaps again, and several people jolt in their seats.

Patrick's eyes narrow at her outburst. "I wouldn't call four women and their unborn children nothing, but no, that's not what I'm telling you. Despite *your* faulty device, Glitch is capable of fixing the camera and retrieving the footage from the rebuilt storage inside."

"Get out, all of you. Leave us." Helena waves her hand, and the five of us slowly rise, and head towards the door.

"Not just them, ALL OF YOU, move!" She shoos her own people out the door behind us. I look back once, and see the room empty except for her and Brock, in the middle of a livid exchange, while he gestures angrily at her.

Thirteen

TROUBLED WATERS

Two days later, the temperature has dropped another ten degrees as the December chill really takes hold. I'm standing at the kitchen sink, hand washing dishes out of boredom, and watching Halle's twins play a one-on-one game of soccer out the kitchen window. Delia does some fancy footwork, zips around Daniel, and shoots a goal into their makeshift net. *Goal. Is the net also called a goal in soccer? I'll have to ask Patrick when he comes back inside.*

A soft tap nearby startles me from my musings, and turning towards the sound, Pierce gives me a small wave from our tiny foyer, standing next to a sleep-mussed Nell. I wave, and he gives me a smile, but it looks off. Not the vibrant Pierce I remember from Georada, with his movie-star flair and his twinkling green eyes.

"I'm going to make coffee," Nell announces grouchily, making a beeline towards the kitchen I just vacated.

"Hey Pierce, is everything okay?" I search his face for hints of trouble, but find nothing obvious there.

He rocks back on his heels, hands in his pockets. "No, it's really not. And there's nobody I can talk to about it, around here. You were always such a good listener, before . . . I thought, maybe, you wouldn't mind taking a walk with me, for old time's sake?"

His uncertainty clenches my heart like a fist. "Of course, Pierce. Let me grab a jacket."

I poke my head out back to let Patrick know I'm going out for a few minutes, and then Pierce helps me slip my arms into the sleeves of my puffiest coat. The Pacific sea air is no joke in winter, even with a buffer distance, like we have here.

We walk for a while in companionable silence, and I keep my hands tucked into my pockets to stay warm. He's sharply dressed in a gray wool coat, and with the wind in his hair, he looks like a gentleman from an old-timey movie.

"So, what do you think of our little city?" he finally asks.

"Well, it's nothing like I expected, though frankly I didn't know what to expect."

He chuckles. "How so?"

How to say it, without sounding so biased? "Everyone's pretty happy here. There are more kids playing in the street than I've ever seen, which is amazing. Everyone shares the community re-sources, *most* everyone is working towards a common goal. There are still issues amongst the families, and Helena . . . well, is Helena. Overall, though, it still feels like a home here."

His eyebrows shoot up in surprise. "It sounds like you actually like it here."

I bobble my head back and forth in indecision. "Yes and no. I'll always miss Jackson Flats, and my family. And my horse—oh *man* do I miss my sweet Morgan." I pause, choking up a little. "But, I can see why you didn't want to give this place up, honestly. You have

110

the freedom to make your own rules, live your own happiness. At times, I admit, it's crossed my mind that life would be simpler if the four of us just stayed here, under the radar." Guilt floods me at the admission, and I look at him out of the corner of my eye to gauge his reaction.

"If only we could go back in time, and make different choices." His wistful words nearly knock me off my feet. Is he saying what I *think* he's saying . . . ?

"What's going on, Pierce?" I don't want to pry, but something's bothering him, or we wouldn't be breathing clouds into the freezing air so he could get it off his chest.

He breathes out through his nose. "Helena's changed. Half the time, she talks and I don't recognize the words coming out of her mouth. The new partner she's accepted, Reave—he's a cold, calculating man. The Helena I met would have never looked at him twice, let alone—" He clears his throat. "I'm just not sure if we're still compatible, after all this time. But if I leave, it's going to cause an uproar. No one has ever left her, and I might be made a pariah."

My stomach knots for him, and I don't have a good answer, only compassion. I reach out and rub his shoulder for a moment in solidarity.

"What do I do, Sadie? You've been through so much, it's deplorable of me to put more on your shoulders. But, you're truly the only person I can ask. Pathetic, isn't it? I wish I'd chosen differently, back then."

Wow, I'm not even sure how to address that.

"Never pathetic, Pierce, but I'm sorry you feel that way." I think it over for a few minutes as we continue our walk, and we've made it further towards the edge of town than I've seen in our time here, twisting and turning down deserted side streets. "Are you sure it's irreconcilable, between you and Helena? I can tell you really care for her, or you wouldn't be so torn up about it."

He stares into the distance, past the buildings and the scrub and the hills. "She used to chase freedom. All of this . . . all of this she scraped together from nothing so that people could be free to live as they chose. It's grown and evolved, sure, but the mission was simple: live free, or die trying. Now, something's different. Instead of freedom, she's chasing power. It's changed her. She's no longer the woman I fell for."

My bones chill at his words, confirming something I've suspected since the first time I met Helena in that air transport she'd abducted us with. Her talk of freedom hides an uglier truth. "Then I think you already know the answer, Pierce. You can't stay with someone you no longer trust and respect, just for fear of others' opinions."

"I think I already knew that," he says quietly, barely audible even over the sounds of our feet on the road. We take another turn and end up at the other side of the open gathering area, finally somewhere I recognize.

"What about you, Sadie? Do you think you might be changing your mind about our poly way of life, here? If you're ready to start looking for husband number two, I'd volunteer in a heartbeat." He gives me a cocky grin, and I smack him on the shoulder.

"No, sorry. And you already know that, Pierce. Patrick is it for me."

He chuckles. "Well, can't blame a man for trying. It's my own fault for letting you go when I still had a shot." He says it with a-good natured tone, and I can tell he's not upset with me for turning down his half-serious proposal.

We walk through the grassy area, meandering in silence. Eventually we end up under a large tree, and the familiar green-and-orange leaves of the magnolia remind me of home. It's out of place here, just like I am, and it brings me a moment of comfort.

"So, enough about me. How are things with you and Patrick? Are you happy?" His tone is decidedly neutral.

"We are, actually. We've had our ups and downs, for sure. But, we're happy. I'm . . . I'm pregnant, actually." I don't know why I tell him, but it feels right.

His face pales, not the reaction I was expecting. "Sadie, that's amazing, but, please, you cannot go around telling people. Have you told anyone else? God, does Helena know?"

Taken aback, I answer, "No. No, I haven't told anyone except Patrick, Atlas, and Nell. I mean, and you, now. But, why are you freaking out right now?"

He rubs his jaw with the heel of his hand, looking stricken. "You'd be a much more valuable target in Helena's eyes, if she knew. Please, *please* don't tell anyone else. You shouldn't have told me."

I don't know what I was expecting when the words slipped out of my mouth, but this wasn't it. "I don't know what to say, Pierce, except that I trust you. If you think it's unsafe to tell Helena, I trust that you won't."

"You're an incredible human, Sadie. Not just your genes, but your kindness, your capability to love others. It would kill me if Helena hurt you. If anyone hurt you." He reaches over and slowly takes my hand. "Congratulations, to you and Patrick. I wish I was half so lucky." The pain in his eyes as he looks away pierces my heart.

"Pierce, why are you so worried about Helena finding out? I don't have any plans to tell her, but even so, what's the big deal? There are several pregnant women here, I saw the list the second day here. Pregnancy shouldn't have anything to do with me being a target. I shouldn't be a target at all, not to our allies." *Supposed allies.*

He meets my eyes warily. "I told you, Sadie. She's changed. You're a polymorph. I'm sure it's crossed her mind that you could advance her genetic testing program. She's nearing forty, and never been able to conceive. It's still possible for her, but she's trying more and more drastic measures to make it happen. A polymorph is already a white whale, but a pregnant polymorph might tempt her to cross the line. Not to mention that your child, *especially* if it's a girl, could be a major target if word gets out of your unique DNA."

With each word he speaks, worry seeps in a little further, and the urge to run builds under my skin like an itch I can't scratch. *Will we truly ever be safe anywhere?* My breaths come faster and faster, and I bolt to my feet.

"Sadie, wait!"

"I have to go."

"Please, Sadie, I won't say anything, I swear!"

"I know, I just have to go. Good-bye, Pierce." I turn and leave him there, sitting in the cold under a lone magnolia in a field of maples.

I burst through the door to our house, nose and cheeks numb from the cold outside.

"Shoot!" Nell sloshes her cup of coffee in surprise from her position on the couch. "Sadie, what's wrong?"

"Nothing! I just want to be alone for a while!"

I shut the door behind myself and crumple onto the bed, my jacket and boots still on. Staring at the ceiling, I hear the couch springs creak, and her footsteps pad across to the sliding glass door. Muffled words filter through, and then her steps approach the bedroom door.

"Patrick got called away by Glitch. Are you sure you don't want to talk to me? I'm a pretty good listener. I might recommend that you have your husband punch Pierce, but I'm not you, so . . . I promise not to judge." She slurps her coffee, and a smile cracks the façade of my shock and fear.

"Thank you, Nell, but I think I'm just going to warm up in the shower. It's too cold here." I heave myself off the bed and feel a twinge in my abdomen. Worry pricks at my mind as I lay my hand across my still-flat belly. *I hope I didn't jostle something in there running back. Oh no, what if something's wrong? I really need to get to a doctor soon.*

With a whole new host of competing worries, I climb into the shower and allow the steaming water to ease the tingling cold from my limbs.

I exit the bathroom to find Patrick once again, but this time he's not waiting for me at the edge of the bed—he's packing a bag.

"Patrick, what's going on?"

"I finally received a location to meet my dad, and we've got to get going." He continues tossing things into the bag as he talks, so we must be on a tight timeline.

I hustle to the dresser and drag clothes on right over my damp hair. "Where do we have to meet him?"

"Northern Manisas. It's close enough to Wrightsville that he won't draw attention traveling there and back, but not close enough to be swarmed by political influences. All things considered, it's a sound choice on his part. It just means we have to leave immediately."

"Okay, fair enough. When are we meeting?"

"Mid-day tomorrow. We need to get there early for Atlas to scout and make sure we have a clear meeting area, and no one follows my dad."

Frowning at that unpleasant possibility, I grab up two days' worth of clothes, and pass them to Patrick to shove into the duffel. "Should I be concerned about that? I know you trust him . . ."

"One hundred percent. I know he would never sell me out, the concern is more about him being followed. Whoever is doing this won't want to be caught out, and we know that. So, we just need to be prepared for as many outcomes as possible. Speaking of which, I think it would be best if you stayed in the security area with Nell and Atlas. I don't like to be separated from you, but I'll have an earpiece so you guys can hear everything, and I think there's less likely to be interference that way."

"Really? Why? You're the prince."

He pauses stuffing the bag with knives for a moment and taps me gently on the end of the nose. "And you're the polymorph."

I shake my head at his goofiness even under pressure. "We are quite a pair."

"That we are. A great pair if I do say so myself." He zips the bag, slings it over his shoulder, and extends his arm to me, as if he's

116

a knight and I'm an elegant lady in the fourteen hundreds, not a modern woman in rumpled black fatigues. So, obviously, I accept.

As he closes the bedroom door behind us, he asks, "Oh, how was your walk with Pierce? Everything okay on that front?"

"Oh, yeah. I'll tell you later."

"Sounds good." He kisses me softly on the temple, yells towards Atlas and Nell's room, "We're ready, guys—we'll meet you at the truck!" and leads me out the front door.

I bury my worries about what Pierce shared for later, when we're not putting out fires with Patrick's father. I need to focus on him right now.

Fourteen

IMPACT

The flight to Manisas was highly boring. Mav is an excellent pilot and, other than the occasional sarcastic commentary over the plane's speakers, she gets us there in a hurry and without incident. Patrick conked out almost as soon as the small plane hit altitude, and I tossed and turned the entire time, restless thoughts souring my chances at a good night's sleep. I couldn't bring myself to dump my latest problems on Patrick's shoulders right before the pivotal meeting with his dad, so I kept them to myself. There will be time later to tell him once this was out of the way. Maybe on the flight home.

Right now, I'm sitting in a folding chair in an empty warehouse catty-corner to Patrick's meeting location with his dad. Atlas has the place wired for sound, and Glitch has set up a portable security monitoring station, so Patrick and his father are covered from every angle. Atlas is currently set up on top of the warehouse next to ours with a sniper rifle and a good view through a large plate-glass window into the chosen building, just in case.

The fact that he feels that's necessary makes me itch. I shift in my seat for the hundredth time in the last half hour, my gritty, sleepless eyes glued to the screen.

"Hold still or I'm going to chop your legs off," Nell grouses, sipping a cup of coffee in the folding chair next to mine.

"I'd listen, Sadie. She threatened to break my tablet yesterday, and she meant it."

"Of course, I meant it, what good is a threat if you don't mean it?" She snorts.

"So, you're going to chop off my legs, and all he gets is a broken tablet?"

"Well, he cares more about his tablet than his legs, so it seemed appropriate."

Glitch rapid-fire clicks on different security camera views and scans them one after the other, never looking our way as he answers, "She's right, I do. I built it myself."

I just shake my head and scooch down in the chair until my braid dangles over the back. The position tugs sharply on some of the strands underneath, but I don't care. I keep my eyes trained on Patrick's stern face. I can see the hope in his eyes, and it's killing me on the inside. *What if his father is guilty, after all? Patrick won't recover from that sort of blow.*

Another hour of waiting passes, and I'm about ready to scream when, finally, there's motion on one of the longer-distance cameras. A sleek silver vehicle pulls up, hovering over the ill-maintained roads at top speeds as it flickers through our field of vision.

"It's time, that's a royal transport from the king's personal fleet."

Leaning forward in my chair, I rub my sandy eyes with the heel of my hand and follow the car's progress as it pulls to a stop right outside the building where Patrick waits. A rear door opens automatically, and I see a more mature version of Patrick climb from the vehicle. His hair is a bit longer, and his crisp suit is something Patrick wouldn't be caught dead in, but the resemblance between the two of them is uncanny. King Royce straightens the cuffs on his jacket, and then strides toward the door of the building with purpose.

He pulls it open, and stands stock still, scanning the building until he spots Patrick, and his shoulders immediately droop with relief. Making all haste, he crosses the room, and my eyes tear up as he throws his arms around his son and wraps him in an enthusiastic hug.

"Patrick, it's so good to see you."

"It's good to see you too, Dad." Patrick returns the hug just as fiercely and closes his eyes for a brief moment.

They both straighten, and his father looks him up and down. "I don't like the look of this, son. Those look like Resistance fatigues. What the devil is going on? Did they kidnap you? Your bride?" He cuts straight to the point.

"Yes and no."

The king's face turns red with anger. "Those rotten scum! I'm of a good mind to wipe them off the map. The audacity!" He turns to pace, and I see where Patrick got the habit.

"Let me explain. There's so much more at play here," Patrick says calmly, and his father turns back to face him.

"Please do."

"All is not as it seems with the New Life Program. You know I received a match, and that she's exceptional." He pauses, and his father nods confirmation. "It's like we were made for each other. Well, not everyone was so lucky with their match. One of Sadie's friends, Josephine, is a very strong-willed girl, and got matched

120

with a man she despised. She complained at one of the gatherings and, rather than address her concerns, they dragged her off like cavemen. We were told she was sedated for her safety, but it was like she vanished into thin air."

"That doesn't make any sense—every girl is meant to be given a backup match, in case the first is unacceptable to them. A veto option was built into the program at its inception. It's inhumane to be forced into a marriage with someone you hate."

Patrick nods. "You're right, it was. But the latest round of emergency provisions making the program mandatory simultaneously required marriage to the highest eligibility man, if there was only one."

"No, that can't be right, son. I'd never sign off on that."

"I believe you, but I'm telling you it's true. I'll send you a copy of the document."

"Please do, we must correct that at once." He runs an agitated hand through his hair. "What does this have to do with your kidnapping? I fail to see the connection."

"Ahh . . . it goes back to Josephine."

"It's always about a strong-willed woman, in my experience." The king sighs in resignation.

"After she was pulled from the meeting, it was like she vanished into thin air. Sadie asked to visit her, but was stonewalled. Eventually, they told us they moved her to another facility."

"Well, perhaps her secondary match was located in another tri-state? I could look into it for you."

"No need, we already found her. Before I explain, I need to show you something." Patrick pulls a rolled piece of paper from his back pocket. "Do you recognize this?" He hands his father the copy of

121

the document authorizing the building commission for the secret research facilities.

"How the devil did you get your hands on this?" he asks sternly. "This is classified." He scans it briefly before looking back at Patrick.

"So, you know what it is?"

"Of course I know what it is, but you shouldn't. Not yet, anyways. Eventually you'll go through an entire transition plan once you're settled and ready to begin your training."

Patrick's face tightens in disbelief, but he presses on. "Can you tell me what it is now, please?"

"Well, the cat's out of the bag, I suppose. As you probably recall, the honeymoon resorts were funded as a result of a single large donor's final bequest. However, the trust is still managed by a legal group, and the *key* requirement of that trust is that any and all negative environmental impact caused as a result of the resorts must be offset. If we should fail to comply, we will revert control of the properties to the trust, and the current legal heirs of the beneficiary. To prevent that happening, next to every single resort, an Environmental Impact Center was built. They are fully staffed with scientists, monitoring equipment, and anything those scientists determine is needed to protect the surrounding environment based on their readings. The budget is absolutely *ludicrous*, but the cost to replace those centers would be higher, so we abide by the plan."

Patrick's shoulders sag with relief. "They're supposed to be monitoring the environment? That's it, you're sure?"

Patrick's father levels him with a steady gaze. "Of course, son. I signed this as part of a package of Environmental Impact guarantees provided by the donor's trust, years ago. This was the hook that came with all the flashy bait. Although at this point I'm more concerned about how you were able to get your hands on it, and if there's a leak in my office, or the trustee's office."

"We've got bigger problems, Dad."

"There are always problems in this line of business, son, you'll learn that soon enough. Now, again, I beg you, tell me what the EICs have to do with your disappearance? And is your lovely bride okay?"

"Sadie's fine for now, Dad. But, those are not EICs. They may have sold them to you that way, but that's not what they've been used for. They're essentially medical research detention facilities. Here, I don't have all of the footage yet, but this was taken inside of one in the past week."

He pulls a small device from a cargo pocket and passes it to his father. The sound of boots running plays over our speakers, and even though I can't see the screen, the look on the king's face says it all when the women are displayed.

Horror washes across his face, and in that instant, I know that he's innocent. "Good, holy God. Are these women ill? Why wasn't I told? What's the meaning of this?!" His voice rises at the end.

Patrick's voice remains calm. "Dad, that's what I'm trying to tell you. Those facilities you signed off on—they aren't being used as intended. Sadie's friend Josephine was taken from a normal meeting at the NLC for 'acting out,' and instead of being taken to a veto match, she was drugged, and disappeared. With the help of a friend, we followed her trail from Georada to Mairmont, and we chose it for our honeymoon in hopes of finding her there happy and well. Instead, she was nowhere. We searched for weeks and eventually found a facility in the woods, a short distance from the main resort buildings. Inside, we found women sedated, pregnant, and strapped to beds. Josephine wasn't given a veto match, she was sedated, and inseminated. She's still there, as far as I know. We weren't able to get her out because we didn't know what she'd been drugged with, or what would happen to all of the other women once the people behind this knew they'd been discovered."

His father's face pales. "Who could do such a thing? It's abominable." He looks shaken, and after a moment sees a bench on the far wall, walks to it, and sits down heavily. "Let me guess, you're here today because you think I authorized this travesty?"

"No, but I had to know for certain. This has to be stopped."

"Immediately," his father agrees.

"I'm glad you think so. We need your help with something. We raided another center this week, and obtained that footage. We were able to rescue the four women inside, before destroying the building. However, one of them is in critical condition, and the doctors available to us haven't been able to wake her. Do you have a physician you trust who might be able to help her?"

"I will see to it immediately. Of course, that means you'll have to tell me where you are."

Patrick grimaces. "I can't. That's one of the conditions of our being allowed to stay. However, we're working with Atlas's people to procure and stock a safe house in western Colkanska, where we could safely bring her and meet your specialists. Do you think you could make that work?"

"I'll make it work if I have to walk into our chief of surgery's office and convince him myself," he vows in a hard tone.

"Hopefully he'll be happy to do a favor for the king," Patrick says wryly.

Patrick's father shakes his head sadly before answering, "I never wanted to be king, son. And I never wanted you to be forced into a life you don't want. Yet here we are. And I'm afraid the people need us even more than I knew." He glances back down at the now-lifeless video player in his hands, looking sick at the memory.

"There's more to do than help this one woman, son, if half of what you've said is true, there are many more than need to be saved. What can I do to aid you?"

"Nothing yet. You can't tell a soul about this, until we find out who's behind it, and who the leak is. If you signed this years ago, and the trust is involved, this goes deeper than even we expected. We have to root out the source, or they'll just continue to work underground. We'll have the safe house ready in forty-eight hours."

"I'll have your doctor there, but I won't just sit on my hands, Patrick. This injustice must be dealt with swiftly," his father argues.

"I agree, Dad, and we're working as hard as we can to stop this. I've got the best people in the world on it as we speak."

His father gets back to his feet and passes the device back to Patrick. "I don't say it enough, but I'm proud of you son. It took courage to confront me, but then, you've always been courageous when it comes to living your own life. You have one week before I step in. Don't let me down."

"I won't. Thanks, Dad." They embrace again, and a single tear escapes and rolls down my cheek. I quickly swipe it away, and realize I'd been holding my breath as I watched their exchange.

Patrick's face on the camera looks mournful as he watches the king exit the building and climb back into the waiting hover car, which zips away as soon as he shuts the door. With his back ramrod straight, he walks to the exit himself.

"It's time for the next phase, team," is all he says, and the staunch determination in the set of his jaw makes me proud to call him mine.

FIFTEEN

DRAWING BOARD

F rom our kitchen back in the Resistance compound, I hear the men's voices as they argue over—I mean, *discuss*—what our next steps should be. With the king's innocence proven—at least to us, if no one else, yet—we're back to square one on who's behind it all. The trust and current heirs are a good lead, but Glitch is pulled between rebuilding the video footage we need as our foundational proof, and trying to simultaneously track down this mysterious trust, and who the beneficiary is. Meanwhile, Helena and crew are breathing down our necks for repaired footage, and information on the meeting with the king, which Patrick has refused to provide.

I stir the vegetables in our borrowed skillet, mulling it over in my mind. The person orchestrating this has to be close to the king, but not in the ultimate position of power they crave. The next possible layer of people would be the queen, assistants, and office personnel, and then his fellow politicians. But my mind keeps fixating on the queen for some reason. She's been so cold in the few interactions I've witnessed. Something about her reminds me of Helena, frankly.

When news of our marriage leaked, she knew. When we were pushed to do that awful interview, she knew. It could be personal bias, or she could be involved. I'll have to ask Patrick later.

"Dinner's ready!" I yell, suddenly too tired to walk all the way to the living room if I don't have to. This baby is sucking the energy out of me at a rapid pace these days, but the nausea has mostly passed, which is nice. Nell volunteered to cook, but so far she's only managed to serve us a charred roast, so I've been giving her cooking lessons in our spare time. Her aunt and uncle never much cared what the kids ate, so most of her childhood with her cousin was spent eating out of graham cracker boxes and fruit packets when available. *I will throttle those useless people if I ever get my hands on them.*

Nell bustles in first, smile wide. "It smells delicious, Sadie. She grabs a plate from the stack on the counter, and starts spooning food out while I settle in at the island to rest. "Did you four make any headway? It sounded heated in there."

"Not heated," Patrick says mildly as he walks in next. "Just trying to work out the best way forward. Glitch has almost got the footage fully restored, but we're not going to share that tidbit yet. Until we know who's behind this, we can't trust anyone. The only two leads we have are the mystery trust, and that the person has access to my father."

"Which is why we landed on setting a trap and seeing who falls into it," Atlas states from his place behind Nell at the stove.

"A trap? What kind of trap?"

He shrugs. "Probably information. Maybe a short clip of the footage makes its way onto the king's desk, and we offer the rest in exchange for money. We'd be betting that whoever's stealing information finds it, but it's all we've got until Glitch cracks the trust. Plus, the trust could be legitimate, and just another tool used by this mole, whoever that may be."

The possibilities make my head hurt. "Well, that sounds like a good plan. But what if they don't want the footage? They can take new footage of the facilities any time they want."

"Well, we were discussing a second option that they might find more enticing—" Atlas begins.

"But it's not an option," Patrick growls.

I narrow my eyes at the two of them. This must have been what they were fighting about. "What is it?"

"It doesn't matter, because it's not on the table," Patrick insists, accepting a plate from Nell.

"Would you two knock it off? It's you, Sadie," Nell says with a bored tone. "Atlas thinks that if we pretend you're blackmailing the king, and you'll be the one to bring the footage, that they'll risk coming to pick you up."

I groan. "Seriously? I am so sick of all of this." I drop my head into my hands and allow myself a momentary pity party. "I'm just one person. I'm not a polymorph, a princess, a genetic prize, a broodmare, or a royal. I'm me. Sadie Ann Taylor Royce. That's it. That's all I want—to be normal. And I want french fries."

Patrick sets the plate of food in front of me, and slides both of his arms around my waist. Even sitting at the counter, he's tall enough that I fit beneath his chin, and I tuck myself into his chest. "I hate to break it to you, but you've never been normal." He drops a little kiss on the top of my hair, and I ignore his words in favor of listening to his steady, calm heartbeat. "You've been extraordinary from the start. I knew it the moment I laid eyes on you in that hallway at the NLC. Before I knew who you were, or about your stellar genes." He drops another kiss. "You've always been someone special to me. Which is why you're not doing this."

I sit back and narrow my eyes at him accusingly. "You're trying to sweet talk me into sitting this out, aren't you?"

"Not at all. I'm flat-out saying no. It doesn't have to be you this time. You're pregnant, and exhausted. Why risk it if we don't have to?" His tone brooks no argument, but I'm not backing down.

"Well, someone has to go, do they not? I assume you're not going to give our footage to somebody in the Resistance to possibly spread around or hand it off to the media to start a smear campaign which would put the women at risk."

"No, of course not," he agrees.

"And you all agreed after talking it through that me going is the absolute highest likelihood that the person we're after is going to show up?"

He refuses to answer, which means yes. I turn to glance at Atlas. "I'll do it."

Rather than answer me, he slides his gaze over to Patrick's and back. "I'll let you two talk it over." He takes a plate from Nell, dropping a kiss on her waiting lips in the process, and exits the kitchen. Glitch hurries to do the same, shooting me a sympathetic look over his shoulder as he leaves.

Nell is the last one—she grabs a plate for herself, and a second one, which she slides in front of the seat next to me for Patrick. "Don't kill each other. Remember, you like each other most of the time."

I snort, and Patrick shakes his head at her as she sashays out of the room.

"Sadie, please, please don't insist on doing this. I understood the last mission because we all had to go. But, I couldn't bear it if you did this and I lost you and the baby. Let Atlas do it. Heck, let me do it!"

My lips press into a thin, annoyed line. "It's no better for me to lose you, or Nell to lose Atlas, Patrick. One of us is going to be taking the risk. Not to mention, I don't think anyone will believe you want to blackmail your dad. Isn't it well known that you two get along well? I'm just the hick from Georada who got a golden meal ticket and tried to cash it in early. Plus, of the four of us, I'm the only one with the genes they want bad enough to take the risk for."

He runs a hand through his hair in frustration, dinner plate ignored. "One, you are not a hick. Two, you're probably right that it can't be me."

"I was just making a point. The whole world sees me as this interloper who lucked out and won the genetic lottery to get matched with the prince. Atlas is the head of an intercontinental security firm, and nobody knows who Nell is—at all—so she would have no motive to try to blackmail the king. It has to be me, Patrick. Honestly, tell me you can see that?"

"You're wrong—it could be me," Glitch says from the doorway, and I startle. I hadn't even heard him come back in. "I can claim to have hacked the footage, and I know Patrick well enough from working with him to have convinced him into a trap and kidnapped you both. They can look me up in their system and see we worked together for years. Went on leave together. It fits. Maybe it's enough if they *think* I have you."

"Glitch, you don't have to do that," I protest.

He waves me off, determination in his eyes. "Neither do you. I'm always the one at the back of the pack, but I can do this. Please, *trust* that I can do this."

Patrick doesn't say a word, just stares at me, putting the decision on my shoulders. I fidget with the end of my braid, thinking over what he's said. "That's very brave of you, Glitch. But I don't think it's enough." His shoulders sag, but I keep talking, "I think you'll need *proof* that you've kidnapped us." He straightens in surprise. "I think I'll need a visit to the medical center . . ."

That night, I lie in bed staring at the ceiling as Patrick finished his shower. One hand on my belly, one hand under my pillow. He opens the door with one towel tied around his waist and drying his hair with another. Satisfied with his hair, he hangs that towel over the doorknob, and comes to lay on his side of the bed. "Penny for your thoughts?"

I'm quiet for a long moment, trying to find a way to express what I'm feeling. "I don't want to sound ungrateful."

He chuckles. "Sadie, just tell me. Whatever it is, good or bad." He rolls to his side and props himself on his elbow to get a better look at my face. It's an impressive display of muscle, and I get distracted for a moment, just taking him in.

"Sometimes, I just want to be normal again. I wasn't joking, earlier. I know it doesn't help to throw a pity party, but don't you ever think about it, Patrick? What would life be like if we just stayed here?"

His eyebrows shoot up in surprise, but he lets me talk.

"I know we have responsibilities, but, if things are going to change anyways, maybe it doesn't have to be *us* who bears those responsibilities. We could just be you and me. No expectations, no political games, no pressure." I sigh, knowing it's not realistic even as I say the words. "It's not home, and Helena's a pain. But the people are nice and friendly. They're normal people, even if they live a different way than we do. Not one person has tried to pressure us, or butt into our family. They've just accepted us as we are. No expectations. When is the last time that has happened for either of us?"

"Be honest with yourself, Sadie. You know there's no way you could deal with Helena permanently. You look like you want to strangle her every time you're in the same room together," he says dryly.

"Okay, so maybe not here. I'd miss my family too much, anyway. But back in Jackson Flats, it could. We'd have family there, and friends if Nell convinced Atlas to go back."

He reaches out for one of my hands, and I give him the one under the pillow. He slowly runs his fingertips along my palm, soothing me with the simple touch. "I have thought about it. What it would be like, if you were a normal girl, and I was a normal boy. And we fell in love two hundred years ago, before any of this mattered. It would have been a gloriously simple life. Because I believe we'd still find each other, in any time, in any life. But this, right here and now, is the life we were given."

I let his words sink in, and deep down I don't disagree. "Do you have to accept the throne? In the past, there were ways someone could step down. Just because your father accepted the throne, doesn't mean you have to, right?" My voice comes out small, quiet in the dark.

"I'm sure there is a way." His voice is hesitant, telling me all I need to know.

"I understand." I try to sound light, and airy, even though it feels like a lead weight has been tied around my neck, and I've been tossed into the deep end of a pool. *The life you knew is gone, Sadie. There's no use wishing for something different now.*

"We don't have to decide any time soon. My father is still a young man, in good health. He'll rule for years before we would be expected to step up. By then, we'll know the right thing to do."

"I hope so," I whisper as he climbs from the bed to don his pajamas, but he doesn't hear me.

Sixteen

MED CHECK

We're up before dawn to start the journey to the safe house, so Paige can meet the king's doctors. Mav looks solemn as they load the heavily pregnant woman on a stretcher into her aircraft, not making a single wisecrack as we load behind them. Patrick is last in line to board, and Mav puts out a hand to stop him before he can climb the steps. I stop and turn, halfway up, to hear what she has to say.

"This is a real' good thing you're doing, hea'. I know they gave you a hard time, but that poor baby's real' sick, and I'm proud to help y'all today." Her voice cracks at the end, and it's the first hint of emotion I've ever seen from her.

"I feel the same way, Maverick. We appreciate your help, and we're glad we can help at least this one mother and child. Hopefully soon we'll help them all."

She nods. "Well, a'right then. Let's go get her some help." Patrick gives her a smile and nod in return, before boarding the plane.

Without further ado, Mav brushes past us to the front, and shuts the cockpit door behind her. A moment later the engines hum to life, and her voice flicks over the speaker. "Somebody holler when the patient is secure for takeoff."

I sit next to Patrick in one of the far back seats, and as we buckle in, he says, "She's good people."

"That she is," I agree.

We watch in contemplative silence as the two doctors in ubiquitous black hover around her, checking vitals and securing machinery for the flight. After what feels like an eternity, they're satisfied. One settles in at her head, and straps into a harness while the other raps twice on the cockpit door before coming back to settle in towards the middle of her gurney, which I can now see they attached to a permanent anchor in the floor of the plane.

Mav wastes no time in getting us airborne, and the now-familiar lurch stays with me long after we've left the ground. Thankfully, it's a short flight to Colkanska, and Patrick thought ahead and procured me some of the lemon-ginger soda that I fell in love with back at the Missiana safe house. I sip it slowly, savoring the flavor and listening to the beep of medical equipment over the steady drone of the airplane. We've been on a lot of flights, but this is the most somber our team has spent together. I send up a silent prayer for the doctors to help Paige when we arrive, and close my eyes, soda resting on my knee.

Not two minutes later—or so it seems—Patrick gives my shoulder a gentle shake. "What is it? Just resting my eyes until we land," I mumble.

"Sadie, we already landed, and they've unloaded Paige. We've got to move to the van."

I rub my eyes groggily. "Okay, I'm coming." I try to stand, but in my sleep-addled state I forget that I'm buckled in. "Oof, ow."

He chuckles. "Hang on, speedy." I feel the backs of his knuckles as he patiently unbuckles me, and then offers me a hand up, which I gladly accept.

With a sigh, I follow him off the plane. A mid-sized white transport awaits us, with a different set of medical staff already waiting to take over Paige's care, just as Atlas arranged. There's an open space in back where she's placed, and they hover around her gurney, taking vitals. Patrick leads me to the front, which has normal passenger seating, and an already-snacking Nell.

"Good morning, sunshine!" she sing-songs, and I shake my head at her.

"Just wait until it's your turn, Nell. And I'll remember this constant cheeriness."

She snorts, "I'm pretty sure we'll be honeymooners forever, right MM?" She elbows Atlas, and he shrugs one shoulder without concern. "Not everyone is fertile Myrtle like you, and I'm okay with that—I've got other plans."

My interest is piqued. "Oh, yeah? What kind of plans?"

She blushes. "Well, I think I'd like to be a doctor. Atlas says he could get me training, even though I haven't had a baby yet. Or, you know, that you and Patrick might grant me a waiver? No pressure, I mean. I get that there's rules, and you can't give me special treatment. But, if I pass all the classes Atlas can get me, I'll have proven that I'm capable by then, and might be eligible for a work study waiver." She rushes through the last part, as if she expects us to laugh at her.

I look at Patrick. "Is that a thing we can do? Give waivers, so women can study what they want?"

He nods in confirmation. "Usually, there has to be a specific reason, such as a death in the family with no other heirs to take over a business that's necessary for a community's survival. However, there are workarounds, especially if a woman shows an exceptional aptitude for an in-demand profession, and her husband doesn't object."

I shoot him a dark look, and he quickly amends, "Not my rule, just stating it as I remember."

Looking back at Nell, hope mixed with disappointment in her expression, dishwater-blonde curls still in a wild tangle from our early morning, I make a snap decision.

"Nell, I hereby grant you a waiver to study the profession of your choosing, at the time of your choosing. You've more than earned it, and if your husband objects I'll kick him in the kneecap." I wink at Atlas, who's unconcerned by my threat.

"Uhm, it doesn't sound like you're allowed to do that, Sadie," Nell points out.

I turn back to Patrick. "That rule was from before there was a monarchy in the North American Alliance, right *Prince* Patrick?"

"Err, yes?"

"Correct. It can be my first official act as a royal. Nell, you can study whatever the heck you want. And if anybody doesn't like it, tell them to talk to me about it."

Her grin spreads ear-to-ear, and she bounces in her seat for a second. "Oh, my gosh, you are such a cool bestie. Can you rule anything you want? Because I've got *ideas*," she says heavily, with a wink.

I roll my eyes at her insinuation. "No, I think this will be a worthy-causes-only sort of situation."

Atlas trades a weighty glance with Patrick before tipping his head in my direction. "You cool with this turn of events?"

He gives me a long look, and I know he's remembering our talk last night, and I feel instantly bashful at my sudden change of heart. "Yep, one hundred percent okay with it. She won't abuse it." He kisses me on the top of the head, and hands me another soda.

Nell instantly starts rattling off all of the training classes she wants to take and talking about how cool it is watching the doctors working with the pregnant women. Her happiness and excitement are infectious, and I smile as she talks our ears clean off. Before long, she's convinced Glitch to hack into the National College database, to get her a list of courses to become an obstetric specialist.

Maybe this royalty thing won't be so bad, after all.

***

The safe house is teeny tiny. It's only got one bedroom, one bathroom, and a large open living area which Atlas's team has turned into a miniature hospital over the last few days. It's impressive what they've pulled off, so far off the beaten path. The king's doctor is poring over Paige's chart and checking the recordings on all of the machinery she's hooked to. We've been here nearly two hours, and he hasn't touched her yet except to take her vitals when we first arrived. Mav and the Resistance doctors are probably already back at their compound by now.

I heave a sigh, and stare back out the window. It's flat as a pancake here and it reminds me of home, except the trees are all wrong. Back home it's all pines and palms, not whatever these trees are.

"Okay, I believe I have a diagnosis, but further testing will be required to confirm it. Due to the extended period of time she's been receiving the paralytic medication, it has suppressed her natural responses indefinitely."

That doesn't sound good. "Can you help her?"

He looks grim. "The exams so far are inconclusive. We'll need to do extensive testing to see if we can get micro-responses to stimuli before pushing a full round of reversal medication. The normal reversal tried by your counterparts wasn't incorrect, just insufficient. Her utter lack of response isn't a good sign. However, we've got a more pressing matter to attend to; she'll be ready to deliver this baby sooner than we'll be able to complete the necessary tests and treatment to wake her. Given her lack of response to stimuli, we'll need to surgically deliver the baby. I need to know how you'd like to proceed with care of the child, and—"

My guts twist, and I suddenly feel hot. "I— I'm going to go take a walk." I dart out the door, without waiting for an answer from anyone.

I walk among the thin-barked trees, and do my best to block it all out. Apparently, when the going gets too real, I need to walk it off. Staying in that room and listening to the doctor cordially lay out how he was going to cut her open and remove the baby she had no idea existed . . . well, it was too much. I lay a hand on my own stomach, and worry floods my thoughts.

How am I going to protect my own child from this same fate? If it's a boy, he'll rule the world one day, but if it's a girl, Patrick's title won't matter one bit. She'll still be expected to marry and have babies and get matched to a stranger one day, when she's old enough. Assuming we manage to protect her, and what will undoubtedly be rare, pure genes. She'll be hunted, just like I've been.

Resolve hardens in my chest. No, *she won't*. If I have to become queen myself to change things, I won't let this happen to her.

Turning on my heel, I march back to the tiny safe house with new steel in my spine. For myself, I might not want a crown. But for my baby? I'd walk through hell and back without blinking an eye, and I hadn't even met him or her yet.

I let myself back in the front door, and Patrick looks relieved to see me. I cross to his side and give his hand a reassuring squeeze. The doctor is still talking, but it seems like they've finished discussing Paige's care, and moved onto Nell asking about his training. I stifle a smile at her enthusiasm.

"Excuse me, doctor?"

He turns to face me. "Yes, Sadie, is it?"

"Yes. Do you think—" I pause, finding the words hard to say in the moment. "Do you have what's needed here to do an initial pregnancy health check?"

"Of course. We have everything needed here to care for any stage of pregnancy, per the king's orders." He gestures vaguely at the wall of gleaming white machines lined up against the pale yellow wall.

"Fantastic. When you're done with Paige's care, would you mind checking me out? I'm pregnant, and we haven't been able to do any of the initial tests yet. We'd just like to know the baby is healthy, and everything is progressing well, if possible."

His gray eyebrows nearly shoot off his forehead in surprise. "Why, of course. As I discussed with the rest of your party, we won't be delivering the baby right away. So, now is as good a time as any. If I'm not mistaken, you're the king's new daughter-in-law, correct? He didn't mention this joyous news."

Patrick interjects, "He doesn't know yet, and we'd appreciate you keeping this to yourself for the time being."

"Of course, sir. Doctor-patient confidentiality still applies," he says tightly. When no one says anything further, he gestures to a chair next to the wall of machinery. "Let's get started with a blood draw. Are you squeamish?"

Oh boy.

SEVENTEEN

EGRESS

"You and the baby are both healthy, according to everything we can tell at this stage," the doctor says, snapping off his gloves. "Congratulations. This is excellent news for you both, as well as the entire NAA."

Relief floods my limbs, and I gaze up at Patrick to see a matching expression on his face. The smile he gives me is huge, stretched ear-to-ear.

One of the machines behind the doctor dings, and he turns, and presses a button. "Ahh! Your blood tests are finished, too. Would you like to know the sex of the baby?" He turns back toward us with a smile.

"Yes!"

"No!" Patrick and I blurt at the same time.

Nell hollers from the seats across the room, "I vote yes!"

"You don't get a vote, Nell," Atlas says blandly, saving us the trouble.

"Rude," she says, but doesn't look offended. She's still too hopped up on excitement about training to be a doctor.

A knock on the door saves us from continuing the discussion, and the doctor's face falls. "Perhaps another time. You have my contact information if you decide you'd like to know."

Atlas crosses and opens the door, letting in the secondary medical staff. "Our transport back to the airstrip is ready, if you two are done?"

Patrick looks at me, before nodding. "Yep, time to head back. Paige is in good hands." We all turn to look one last time where she's laid out on the bed, still asleep.

I walk to her side one last time and give her hand a squeeze and lean down to whisper in her ear, "We're doing our best for you, Paige. Fight to meet your baby. Fight to wake up, you're safe now." I run a hand across her hair, smoothing it away from her face, and for a moment, it seems like one of her eyes twitches, but then nothing.

I place her hand gently back on the bed beside her and follow our group back out to the white transport, and back to reality.

Five minutes later, we're on the road and discussing Paige's future.

"It sucks he couldn't wake her up. I thought as a specialist he'd be able to wave a magic wand."

Glitch snorts. "He's a physician, not a magician."

"But still, he's the top of his field. It's just a letdown. It's depressing to think even when we get them out, they still may not get to live their lives again. I wanted all four of the women we saved to be saved, that's all."

"I did too, hon," Atlas murmurs.

The rest of the transport ride is a somber affair, with each of us lost in our own thoughts. It's so bittersweet. Our baby is healthy, and I feel like I can breathe a huge sigh of relief. But my heart hurts for Paige, and I can't help but go down the terrible rabbit hole of how many more women we may rescue, only to be too late.

We pull up at the airstrip, and all pile out to find Mav's out of the cockpit and checking something on the front of the plane.

"Everything okay, Mav?" Atlas calls out when he notices her eyeing the nose of the aircraft.

"Yeah, I think it'll be okay, we smacked a bird on the way back, just doing an extra preflight to make sure there's no damage. The plane does it automatically, but I'm old-fashioned. Jus' like to be thorough when you're going to be in the air. It ain't a car, you can't just pull over if there's a problem."

"Well, this day keeps getting better. Poor bird," Nell mutters darkly.

"I know. How often do you think that happens?" I ask, never having considered it before.

Atlas crosses to her side, to join her in checking the plane over, and the rest of us take the moment to stretch our tired limbs.

"How is it that the less you do, the more tired you are?" I ask Patrick.

He chuckles. "It's been an emotional day. That takes it out of you."

"True," I agree, giving him a small smile. He snags me around the waist and leans in for a kiss.

"Patrick, there are people here." I give him a playful smack on the shoulder, and he grins at me happily. It's infectious, and I grin right back at him.

"I don't care," he says simply, and kisses me right there on the tarmac. Within a heartbeat, I get lost in him, completely forgetting the people, the cold, the long, emotional day. All I know is Patrick, and his lips warm on mine, and tingles down to the tips of my toes.

"Lovebirds, get your feathered butts over here before Glitch has a conniption." Nell interrupts our bubble of happiness and, after lingering in each other's arms a moment more, we both turn in her direction, at the base of the plane's stairs. Glitch does indeed appear troubled as he futzes with another little device, one we haven't seen before.

Atlas looks confused as he walks back from the front of the plane, leaving Mav to finish the inspection alone. "What's a conniption?"

Nell rolls her eyes to the heavens. "Seriously? What is with you northerners? A conniption! You know, a fit. A freak out. A call-the-people-with-butterfly-nets moment? I really have to get this one home to Georada for an education when this is all over with," she says to me while pointing at him with her thumb, and shakes her head in bemusement. He actually looks sheepish, and it's adorable.

Patrick and I have made it to the base of the stairs, and Glitch sighs in relief. "Good, we don't have time to mosey, people. Nell, quit hassling your husband and get up here. I need to turn on the sound blocker, and your elementary flirting can wait."

My eyebrows nearly fly off my face, they shoot so high. Glitch is never that snippy, even in the middle of an operation. As soon as we're all inside the cabin, he presses the lone button on the top of a small blue device, and a blue rectangle of light shoots out onto the curved wall. Atlas hustles over and snatches the window cover down, so the shot is clear. When Nell closes the door, he presses the button on his favorite noise blocker before pressing the blue button again on the projector.

Where before there was a blue square, a live feed of the Resistance's conference room, Helena on the far left of the screen, pops into place. Noise comes from the device, and she's droning on about fuel cell locations. Brock looks murderous, and some sort of green blob is in the upper right corner.

Atlas's voice is wary, "Glitch, what did you do?"

"Hold on, they've already changed subjects. They're just going over their next supply run route now. That's not the problem." The images on the screen flicker rapidly as he taps on his tablet like a demented chicken. "Ahh, here. *This* is the problem."

The image snaps back into place, and he grumbles under his breath, "I can't believe my aim was off. Now we're going to have to watch everything to the left. So annoying."

"How did you even do this, Glitch?" Patrick interjects his ramble to ask.

"Oh, remember when I knocked over the plant a while back? Well, I had a feeling they were up to something fishy, so I planted a little trinket into the pot when I shoved the soil back in. It's blackish brown, so it's really hard to spot in the middle of dirt. Invented it myself!"

"Glitch, shh." Nell bats a hand in his direction, eyes riveted to the makeshift screen where Helena is speaking.

"It's obvious they're making an exit strategy—I don't buy for a minute that this little *health mission* today was all humanitarian. There's only one known polymorph on the planet, and you think we're just going to let this opportunity pass by? No. We need eyes on them around the clock when they're back, and we have to get her into our testing program. No more of this catching us by surprise and running off to meet with the enemy and plotting their own safe houses. We need them here, where we can keep an eye on them. Besides, our scientists are just as good as those at the NAA, there's no reason we couldn't leapfrog them, and make a breakthrough sooner. We need as much genetic material as we can get." Helena's words shouldn't shock me, but they hit me like a lightning bolt to the core, nonetheless. Cold feels like it's seeping up from my toes as she laughs. "Can you imagine if we got an egg or two? God, the genetics lab could have a field day with that. A couple of super-eggs, our best sperm donor, and we'd be set. Nobody would catch our research team, and when we had the science on our side, we could take the entire *Americas*." A slow grin crawls across her features, and I begin to feel faint.

"Somehow I think the sperm donor you've got in mind might protest, given recent events," Brock says bitterly, and I realize they're talking about Pierce. My stomach rolls over into a knot at how wrong it all is. "Also, I think you're forgetting that our genetic testing program is voluntary, and there's no way she'll sign up for it."

Helena's mouth pinches angrily at the reminder of her no-longer-lover, and she narrows her eyes at him. "Voluntary for Resistance members, but I think it's about time our *guests* contributed something to the cause, don't you? If she doesn't volunteer, we'll just make her do it. She's one girl, and this kind of research is for the good of humanity. Honestly, Brock—I hope you're not going soft on me, are you?" She stares him down in challenge.

He clenches his jaw, and I can see the rage in his steely eyes, but he doesn't immediately respond to her goading.

A voice off-screen says something, but my ears are ringing, and I can't make out the words no matter how hard I try. I sway on my feet. Patrick's voice comes through deep water, and I can't make out the words.

Panicked voices surround me, Nell's higher-pitched voice rising above the rest cuts through, "Sadie, BREATHE."

I suck in a lungful of air, and next thing I know, I'm on my butt in the middle of the aisle, staring up at four very concerned faces.

"Don't you dare pass out; we are not in some lame romance movie!" Nell shakes my shoulder, and I swat her hand away.

"I'm fine, I just lost my balance," I protest, but she just mutters in response.

"That's what I'd say, too," Atlas rumbles in amusement.

Patrick is hovering over me, a concerned look on his face as he extends a hand to help me back to my feet. "I won't let them touch you, Sadie. I swear it. We'll leave right now and come up with another plan to deal with the women in the rest of the facilities on our own. Our safe house is nearby, and my father's on board."

"The butterflies . . ." I whisper, my private name for the women tumbling from my lips.

"Morbid, Sadie." Glitch immediately catches my reference to the bugs pinned on a science board. "But not altogether inaccurate." He pushes his glasses further up his nose with one finger and turns back to the impromptu screen.

". . . we'll have to separate her from the others, but I don't imagine that will be a problem." This time it's Brock who's speaking. "If we have to, we'll invite them along on our next mission, and we'll cause a riot along their route—something big. There's no way the men will agree to let them go once we tell them it's too dangerous, and Branch says her little friend is easily distracted." He snorts. "It's utterly ridiculous. These four are supposed to be the ones rocking the foundations of the government? Hardly. You'll have a new set of puppets, more like. But still, if you get her alone and cornered, she'll probably consent to the testing."

"I always did love dolls, as a girl." Helena looks down at a nail, and picks at her cuticle as if thinking about old times.

"So, the next supply run it is, then. According to her medical file, she should be due for a pregnancy check soon. We'll just tell Prince Charming that he can't take his future offspring into danger." Brock leans back in his chair and flops a booted foot onto the table as if he owns the place.

"You know, I've always wanted to be a mother. Maybe we'll lift the eggs, and I'll be the surrogate. Who's better qualified to raise them? They'll have superior genes and superior training—we'll be able to breed our own super-soldiers." She looks pleased with herself, and I feel the urge to vomit all over the plane.

Her tinkling laugh is joined by several other voices around the room, and the cold I'd felt before is replaced with boiling hot fury.

Glitch taps his screen again, and the image vanishes as quickly as it appeared. "The rest is just more laughing and then they start talking about the riot portion of the plan. I'll spare you the coronaries. Obviously, we need to re-group here."

"Forget re-group, we need to get out. Immediately." Patrick's tone is all business.

"That poses a problem, given that Maverick was going to be our transport. Also, we don't have anywhere to go. Paige is occupying the only safe house we're close enough to reach before we're caught." *Leave it to Atlas to be the voice of reason.*

"Did you not just hear them planning to split us up and perform medical tests on Sadie? Take her eggs, fertilize them, and *implant them into Helena?*" He's yelling, and I lay a calming hand on his arm.

"Patrick, that's not going to happen."

"Good Lord A'mighty, what is going on?" Mav's voice from behind us causes us to turn in horrified unison.

"Mav, how long have you been standing there," Atlas asks slowly, the dangerous undertone in his voice causing the hairs on the back of my arms to stand up.

"Long enough to know somethin' ain't right, and you five are about to do some explainin'." She crosses her arms over her chest and stares us down without flinching. If I wasn't in a full panic, I'd have been impressed by her mettle.

"Mav, this doesn't have to concern you, just let us go, and we'll figure something out." Patrick tries a soothing tone.

"Oh now, you know I didn't just fall off the truck last night. Something's bad wrong, and I ain't moving unless you give me the story. Right here, right now. Because from what I just heard, well, it sounds like the Queen Bee done gone off the deep end. And that's a whole lotta bad for a whole lotta innocent folks, starting with you, Sadie."

We exchange a long glance, and Glitch backs the footage up to the beginning, and presses play again. I close my eyes and breathe through my nose until it's over.

Mav sits down hard in one of the seats, shock plain on her dark features. She tugs lightly at the bottom of her close-cropped curls. "Y'all got a safe place to go? Or did you just give it to that poor sick pregnant woman?"

Atlas's grim expression must tell her all she needs to know because she nods once, sharply.

"A'right then, here's what we're gone' do. You five are going to buckle up, and we're going to fuel up for a longer flight." She gets back to her feet slowly, and gazes around at each of us. "What's the hold up? Sit down, we've got to get a move on! This isn't one of those things you can sit on all day, and hope for rainbows. You gotta move, and move now or they'll be coming after us, and we need a head start."

"Where are you going to take us, Mav? If you don't take us back to Helena, she's going to be after you, too."

"Honey, that's a whole lotta evil. And you five, you're good people. You can't even help yo'selves right now, and you're helping others. I see that, and anybody with a brain in their head sees that. Helena, she's always been something else, but she wasn't evil, not before. What I just saw on that video, that's *evil*. And besides, I know a place, and it sounds like y'all need one to lay up for a while."

Tears prick the back of my eyes, and her unexpected kindness robs me of words. Nell steps forward and wraps her in a hug.

Startled, Mav pats her a few times on the back, wide-eyed. "Okay now, Nell, you go on and sit yourself down. I ain't kiddin', we got to move."

And so, we did.

EIGHTEEN

ZANETTI

W hile grateful to Mav for stepping up, I still had a smidgen of doubt that she'd risk everything to take us to safety. When I woke to Patrick shaking my shoulder and there was nothing out the window but snow and solid ice as far as the eye can see, worry prickled that something had gone horribly wrong. But when she flies us directly over an ice-encrusted volcanic caldera, my jaw drops. "Patrick, where are we?" I rub my eyes, wiping away the sleep.

"Alaska Territories, I think. Just based on the time we've been in the air, and the mountain ranges. You've been asleep a long time."

"Patrick, how are we supposed to survive up here? Back home, the rumors are that the people up here are a little crazy, and there's only one surviving settlement, as far as I know."

"The closers don't come up this far, so they've established their own cities organically," Atlas volunteers. "Not much is known about them, except that they're the last true survivors on the continent. Everyone else has eventually turned to the NAA government for infrastructure aid, but they haven't. It's mind-boggling, given the harsh conditions. It's also, unfortunately, one of the few places I don't already have a contact."

Glitch looks concerned when he asks, "You weren't able to insert someone into their community?"

Atlas snorts in derision, "I wasn't able to *find* their community to insert someone. I'm not convinced a community still exists up here. My best researchers couldn't find a single trace of humanity, let alone reach anyone."

Nerves knot my stomach. "So, where is she taking us?'

As we approach a peak just to the side of the volcano I feel the lurch of descent, and I swallow, my mouth suddenly dry. *If she leaves us out here, it's game over.*

My eyes find Patrick's, and I find my concern mirrored there.

"Holy cats on Christmas, look at that!" Nell exclaims. I whip back around towards the window and can't believe my eyes. As we descend, a gaping maw opens in the side of the peak, snow disappearing through the new opening.

Mav guides us smoothly through the opening, and as we touch-down with a gentle bump the doorway above is already closing over us. Within ninety seconds, everything around is pitch black, and the plane's lights only carry a few feet before the enveloping blackness prevails.

The sound of the cockpit door opening startles us from our shock, and we turn as one to gawk at Mav.

"Where the heck are we?" Nell is the first to ask.

Mav's smile is slow to spread, and she stretches stiff shoulders before answering. "I brought you to meet my auntie."

"Your auntie?" I ask, confused.

"Come on, y'all. You're gone' like her." She presses her hand against the panel that operates the exterior door, and the stairs automatically descend. Without waiting for a response, she plods down into the darkness.

"There's nothing else for it," Atlas says with resignation, and follows her out. My feet have just touched the bottom stair when Mav yells at the top of her lungs, "Auntie, turn on the lights! It's Maverick." The sound echoes dully in the space around us, and it gives me the sense we're in an underground cavern of some kind.

A wizened voice comes from the darkness, the direction unclear. "My niece has a name, but it isn't Maverick."

Mav sighs. "Fine, Auntie. Please turn the lights on, it's *Maeve*," she mutters a curse under her breath at the indignation of having to use her given name.

Lights at floor level flick on all around us, and the actual breadth of the cavern shocks me. There is a full-on airport under here. In my entire life, I've never been inside a man-made space this large. The five of us stand in stunned silence as an older black woman with pure white hair in waist-length braids strides out of the gloom towards us. Her speed belies her apparent age, as she moves with the grace of a much younger woman. A long maroon skirt swishes about her bare feet, and her smile is warm, and genuine as she embraces Mav. *Maeve*.

"Good to see you, sweet niece of mine," she croons, as if talking to a baby and not the capable, formidable woman that I know her niece to be.

Rather than complain, Maeve responds in kind, "It's wonderful to see you, my beautiful Auntie." Exchanging wide smiles, they turn to face us, and I see the strong familial resemblance despite their opposite styles and attitudes.

Mav's auntie strides forward and sweeps her hands out wide at her sides. "Welcome to Zanetti!" she booms, and a thunderous cheer surrounds us, echoes unearthly in the enclosed space.

My grip on Patrick's arm is tight, and I am overwhelmed and awed, unable to speak. Eventually, relative silence returns to the cavern, but the sounds of people can be heard nearby.

"We were not expecting you for months, Maeve. Who are these strays you've dragged to my doorstep?" She inclines her head kindly towards us, taking the sting out of her words.

"Auntie, it's a long story. One we should take somewhere quiet." She drops her voice low, aware of the amazing acoustics in the under-mountain airport. "Besides, these folks have had a real' rough day. They could use some Zanetti hospitality."

"Well, why didn't you say so? Friends of peace are always welcome at our home-fires. Before I grant you access to our home, you must agree to the rules." She continues without waiting for us to respond, "You must walk with peace amongst the Zanetti people; you must leave your knowledge of Zanetti behind you when you go; and you must think first of others, always. If you cannot do this, we will bring you sustenance and send you back on your way with kindness in our hearts." Her pronunciation is firm.

Patrick steps forward and extends his hand to her. "My name is Patrick Royce, and we appreciate your hospitality. On behalf of my party, we accept your terms, and I will add another. We will take nothing from Zanetti that we do not intend to return in kind, when we are able, Mrs. . . . ?" He looks at Mav, who nods in acceptance of his promise.

"You may call me Auntie."

Without missing a beat, Patrick responds, "Thank you, Auntie."

"I should accept nothing less of one of Maeve's strays. And I'm always glad when she brings them to us." She turns and tosses more words over her shoulder as she leads us from the great cavern, and down a gently sloping path. "It's the only way I get a visit, most of the time."

Maeve scoffs, "I fly out here every year. I'm gone' start complaining that you never leave your hill to come and visit me, Auntie."

I loosen the top of my jacket, surprised at the steamy warmth permeating the air. After a moment's indecision, I take it off and sigh at the glorious balminess. I don't know how they've done it, but they've created a blissful cocoon under a mountain range laden with snow. We twist and turn down the gently sloping path, crossing many switchbacks as we descend into the mountain. The weight of the rock above looms, giving me a hint of anxiety if I allow my mind to wander there. Luckily, the sights and sounds here are endlessly diverting, so I don't have time to dwell on it.

We pass countless people, each dressed as brightly as Auntie in loosely flowing garb. Extravagant textiles are only where the rich culture starts, though, as the structure they've carved out of the mountain is a work of art. The ceilings are scraped in mind-bending patterns, no two the same. The walls are embedded with soft lighting, but at the perfect level of brightness to avoid squinting. There are no visible wires, or any hint of how they work. I run my hand over them, and feel no heat from the source, only the natural warmth radiating from the stone.

Many people walk barefoot, and everyone we pass exchanges a greeting with Auntie, Mav, and us—even though newcomers must be incredibly rare here. After an indeterminable amount of time, Auntie leads us into a cozy set of rooms carved into the mountain. There are no man-made walls here, just stone, but they've decorated the room with beautiful linen hangings. The room is surrounded by lush colors, depicting a far-off jungle scene, a great tiger mid-swipe on one, a cherry-red bloom on another. I walk over to the closest one, and lift a tentative finger, and find the fabric is delicate and paper thin. "How old are these?" I ask, scared to breathe on them too hard, for fear of damaging them.

"Good eye, girlie. Those have been in this room at least one hundred years, now." Auntie answers me.

"They're stunning, truly." I back away and realize that we're in more or less an apartment kitchen. A bedroom and bathroom branch off of the main area, and that's about it.

"Thank you, Mrs. Royce. If you like them, this can be your suite for the evening. I'll take the others for some rest as well; we have more rooms just down the hall. One of my people will be along with dinner shortly. In the morning, we'll discuss your options and your plans with The People."

"Auntie, I don't know if that's a good idea . . ." Mav sounds wary.

"Maeve, you know our ways. What is good for the individual must be good for us all. We live as family, decide as family." Without further comment, she turns on her heel and starts down the hall. Mav follows her, heatedly whispering to no avail. Nell gives me a quick side-hug, and then she, Atlas, and Glitch follow after Auntie to their own spaces, shutting a metal door behind them.

I settle onto a carved stone bench, and just stare at Patrick where he leans against the opposite wall, the brightly colored blossom hanging beside him.

"Did you know any of this was here? I'm just so . . . overwhelmed by the enormity of it all."

"I had no idea," he says, "I was told in all of my training that the only thing up here were a few small cities, clinging to existence in a frozen wasteland. This is absolutely nothing like I expected." His tone is reverent, awed at the massive undertaking creating the underground city must have been.

"And their technology is impressive, as well. Their lighting is like nothing I've ever seen. And what do they eat? I'm a bit afraid to see what they'll bring us for dinner," I admit, imagining freezer-burnt polar bear next to a side of . . . well, I don't even know what.

"Forget the food, how are they heating the place? It's downright steamy under here. My thought is, they must have somehow tapped the volcano in the next mountain. They'd have to, right? But I don't see any pipes, vents, or anything. And there's no stench, or fumes."

We both ponder all the marvels we've seen so far, and in no time at all there's a timid knock on our metal door.

I cross to the door and swing it wide to see a tiny young woman with a spray of freckles across her delicate nose on the other side holding a heavy tray. "Good evening. Auntie asked me to bring you both supper. May I come in?"

"Of course. Thank you so much!" I step to the side, and wave her towards the table, where she places the tray with care. As soon as she passes me, the heavenly scent of fresh-baked bread infiltrates my senses.

"We weren't sure what you liked, so we just brought some of everything. But we do hope you enjoy, and perhaps will join us for our family meal tomorrow morning?" She hesitates, as if she isn't sure if she was supposed to invite us.

"We'd love to," I say firmly. *We have to know the people to lead the people. Although it seems these people already have a strong leader.*

She smiles and ducks her head before scurrying out the door, without even telling us her name.

Patrick, unconcerned with her hasty exit, has already removed the lid and is heaping food onto metal plates. There appears to be some kind of barbecued meat, roasted vegetables, and a humongous loaf of crusty bread, next to a crock of pearly yellow butter. It's so cold and fresh, a drop of moisture has accumulated at the top, and rolls slowly down the side to settle in the bottom of the dish.

My stomach rumbles loudly, spurring me to join Patrick at the table, instead of gawking at the delicious spread.

He passes me a plate, and I greedily tuck in. The first bite practically melts on my tongue, and I groan with pleasure. Not a word passes between us until both of our plates are completely cleared, and I'm nibbling on my third hunk of bread slathered in the—slightly tangier than usual, but still delicious—butter.

Patrick offers me the first shower, which I gratefully accept, before changing into a pair of loose linen pajamas—chartreuse, naturally—and fall into the firm bed. The last thing I see before closing my eyes is the beautifully carved stone ceiling, where it seems a hint of tiger's eye is winking at me in the dim blue lighting.

Nineteen

THE PEOPLE UNDER THE HILL

Climbing out of bed is hard in the morning, but Patrick insists that we be good guests, and so we are up, dressed, and presentable when Sheena, our pleasant guide, shows up to lead us to breakfast. The lights are on a cyclical timer to mimic natural daylight; when we'd woken, the pale blue gradually faded into the pale yellow of a weak morning sun. By the time we reach the family dining area, the lights have strengthened significantly.

Sheena leads us to a low, round table towards the center of the area, where we find a tray of steaming food already piled. She instructs us to serve ourselves and scurries off to her other morning tasks.

"I feel bad that we showed up at their doorstep, and they're waiting on us hand and foot," I say between bites.

"I do too, but if we are here more than a day or so, hopefully they won't continue to do that. It's really up to how well Glitch can orchestrate things from here so we can move onto the next phase of our plan."

160

And, speak of the devil, Glitch approaches our table, his usual scattered look amplified by the entire left side of his hair sticking straight up, and his glasses slightly askew.

"Are your ears burning?" Patrick asks as Glitch drops down heavily into the nearest seat.

"No, are yours? Are you having a reaction to something? My ears are fine, but this light is messing with my eyes. It puts a glare on my glasses, and everything is just off for some reason." He shakes his head in bewilderment.

Leaning across the table, I hand him a plate of food, and gently tap the arm of his glasses, so they settle into place. He jolts.

"Whoa, that's . . . better actually, thank you. Maybe I didn't sleep enough last night, after all." He looks sheepish, and shoves a piece of leftover bread into his mouth to cover it up.

The room fills quickly as we eat, and I begin to get a better scale of how many people live in this underground sanctuary. There must be several hundred, at least.

"How many people do you think are in here?" I wonder aloud.

"Two hundred twenty-seven, not counting us," Glitch answers, not having to think about it.

"How do you just know that, man? It's weird," Patrick comments, taking a sip of the strong, dark beverage provided. It's not coffee, but since I don't know what it is, I've opted to skip it.

Mav strides across the room as if she owns it, Nell and Atlas at her side. Once they join us and we're all well satisfied, I notice Auntie across the large dining hall, speaking with people at each table as she slowly crosses the room in our direction. The graceful sway of her skirts matches her unhurried pace, and I have time to study her easy manner from afar.

Eventually, rather than coming to us, she reaches the middle of the room, and steps up onto a single wide circular step. "Good morning, family!" Her voice booms and bounces in the vast space, just like it did in the airport last night.

"Good morning, Auntie!" the people reply in unison, and the power of hundreds of voices as one saturates the air.

She laughs, true joy in the sound. "We have visitors today, for the first time in a long, long while. What say you all, that we hear from them?"

Feet stomp in an increasing rhythm through the room, and after a minute, the floor reverberates with the pounding. My heart thrums faster, caught in the rush . . . and nerves over speaking of our situation with so many people here. What if they kick us out, once they realize how risky it is for me to be among them? Where would we go, when nowhere has been safe?

She raises a hand, and the noise instantly stops. "Who speaks for you, travelers?" she calls, eyes boring into us.

Patrick answers without hesitation, "I do, Auntie."

"Come then, and tell us how you came to Zanetti, and The People under the hill." She gestures to the space next to her on the step, and he crosses confidently to her side. He steps up, and his calm demeanor in the midst of so many searching eyes is reassuring.

"Hello, thank you all for having us in your spectacular home. Your hospitality is exceptional, and I can truly say that I've been all over the world, but there is nothing else out there quite like Zanetti."

The people cheer as one, and the noise deafens me. Auntie gives him an appreciative smile, and he continues. "My name is Patrick Royce, and I'm traveling with my lovely bride, Sadie, and our friends Atlas, Nell, and Glitch. You may know that there have been some changes in the wider world of late."

He pauses, as if considering how best to explain our circumstances. "There have been changes in the laws in many cases, but the two most critical have been that the formerly optional New Life Marriage Program has been made compulsory for all women aged nineteen and older. That is how I met my bride, Sadie, and how Atlas met his, Nell." The three of us wave, and waves sprout back at us like daisies in the summer sun.

"The second is that our governmental structure has been changed, from a democracy to a monarchy. The former prime minister Royce has been made the first ever king of the North American Alliance. He is my father."

He pauses for a moment, to let that tidbit sink in, and it's silent as shock permeates the crowd, and they look at each other with wide eyes.

"However, despite our newfound positions, and the many privileges you can imagine they afford, Sadie and I have found ourselves lacking a key privilege: safety. We are hunted now, by both the NLC program, and likely, the Resistance. Both institutions pledged our safety, but we found them to be deceitful, and covering up much darker truths. One of our acquaintances at the NLC has been drugged, impregnated against her will, and held captive in a secret research facility. The five of us escaped on discovering this, so that we could try to help release the captive women, because to our horror, we found many, many more than just our friend." His face is somber.

"We were taken in temporarily by the Resistance, but their leaders tried to deceive us, as well. And in the end, they wanted to use Sadie for the same purpose as the women we were trying to rescue. If it were not for Maverick, and her boldness in our rescue yesterday, we would, right now, be back in their hands. To

Maverick, we say, thank you for your help in our hour of need, and your willingness to put the needs of others above your own. We will never forget your bravery, and your true friendship." He clasps his hand over his heart and bows deeply at the waist in a gesture of respect.

Maverick, still seated, inclines her head in acknowledgement, but a flush stains her cheeks at being called out so publicly. Patrick turns to Auntie, signaling that he has no more to say.

Rather than make a pronouncement of her own, she turns to the crowd, arms open wide. "What say The People?" she booms once again.

For a moment, painful silence is the only response. But after a moment, an elderly man at the middle of the clustered tables stands painstakingly to his feet with the help of a cane. "They possess the heart of The People, even from afar. Their mission is worthy, and we should support them."

A younger woman across the other end of the great hall stands, and adds her lyrical voice. "We must aid them in their time of need, for none should be refugees for doing what is right."

One after the other, people all over the hall rise, and soundlessly clasp their hands over their hearts. In time, everyone in the room is on their feet. Their approval and acceptance hit me like a brick wall.

"The People have spoken!" Auntie says, and the foot-stamping resumes, shaking the hall, and what feels like the whole mountain. When it subsides many minutes later, she turns to Patrick. "We will support you in your endeavors. Whatever you need, if it is in our power, we will provide it."

Patrick is choked up when he next speaks. "We are in your debt, People of Zanetti. You have our eternal gratitude for taking us in, at this critical moment. We are still working to save the captive women and will likely not be with you for long. But your hospitality will never be forgotten, and we will hold the kindness of your people fondly in our hearts for the rest of our days."

True to their word, we are provided with everything we need to complete our planning and get back on our way as soon as possible. Immediately after the people's approval, Auntie escorts us to a secure room, filled with wall-to-wall tech gadgetry. Glitch's eyes about bug out of his head at the sight, and he quickly befriends the woman in charge of the technological operations that allow Zanetti to function. While he does the important work of re-connecting to civilization and planting the bait for the person behind it all, the rest of us are taken on a tour of the mountain. For a little while, I let myself be immersed in the discoveries and accomplishments, and shelve the trouble waiting for us behind every corner.

The amount of genius tucked into this mountain is awe-inspiring. From their underground herd of musk oxen and their expansive produce farms—which grow with a combination specialty lighting and re-directed sunlight from above—to the sheer skill involved in tapping the volcanic flow of the neighboring mountain for the balmy heat, everything about the place is a wonder. But the people are humble, taking pride in their home with humility in their hearts.

The only person who gave me an answer as to how all of their advancement came to be was an elderly man with a cane who said, "From superior need, develops superior science."

We are trying our hand at spinning musk ox fiber into thread when Glitch arrives, panic plain in his wide eyes and heaving sides. "Guys, something's going down at the Resistance." He gives Atlas a handheld video device, and then bends over to put his hands on his knees and breathe hard.

I set down my tools, the fun of the moment lost as the tinny sound carries across the small space from the device in Atlas's hand. It's the end of the video of Helena talking about running tests on me, and bile rises in my throat. It cuts off, and Atlas questions Glitch in confusion, "What's different, we had this yesterday, did we not? It's why we didn't go home . . ."

"Apologies, yes." He straightens, red as the radishes we just helped pick at the produce farm. "It is the same footage, but not the same source. Once I was successfully reconnected to the web, all of my devices went berserk with Resistance alerts. I *may* have inserted myself into their databases as a permanent resident, so I could monitor their communication channels. Anyways! That footage came through three hours after we first watched it . . . and went to every single resident of the Resistance."

"How did they get it? I thought your camera was untraceable?"

Glitch frowns. "I'm still working on that, to be honest. Either they tapped the camera itself, or intercepted my outbound transmission. I will find out. That's not all, though. Four hours later, another transmission came through." He taps the screen rapidly and passes it back to Atlas. This time, we all gather around him to watch the new footage.

166

Brock's somber face fills the screen, seated at the head of the table in the conference room, in Helena's usual spot. "Brothers and sisters, I have a grave announcement for you today. As you saw this morning, Helena has chosen to cross a line that is unconscionable. Her decision to pursue involuntary genetic testing on someone under our protection is not something that we as the Resistance stand for. As you well know, we founded our city for protection from the kind of oversight and persecution—as enforced by the NLC, and NAA government—that threatened to cripple our freedoms. I cannot personally stand for that, as I know that you cannot stand for it." He pauses, locking his steely gaze on the camera. "That is why I must tell you that Helena has been removed as leader of the Resistance, effective immediately. Your voices were heard today as you made your stand, and we, the remaining leadership team, stand with you in what is right."

"Some of you have asked about the location of Sadie, and the rest of her party, and their safety. I promise you, they have been taken to a safe house, early this morning. Rather than risk Helena's plans, we agreed together that it would be best if they remained elsewhere until the leadership here is fully settled, and we can once again assure their safety as friends and guests of the Resistance."

"What a crock of bullsh—"

"Nell!" I snap. "Shh!"

"Brothers and sisters, I humbly offer myself as a nominee for the permanent leadership role, in place of Helena. I will serve temporarily until the official vote can be organized. All nominees can be recognized this evening in the gathering field, at seven p.m. Let us come together in this time of crisis and rise better than we were before." He nods to the cameraman, and the video cuts off.

I stare, blinking at the now-blank screen in anger. "So, when we didn't show up, they decided to, what, spin it to their own benefit? Throw Helena under the bus, obviously. But for what?"

"Power." Patrick's voice is clipped. "Brock is clearly making a power grab. He's tired of sitting beside Helena, watching her run things." He gestures angrily as he speaks.

Atlas grunts agreement. "It's definitely a power play. But what's he going to gain when we don't show back up as promised?" His tone is cryptic, and it makes the hair on the back of my neck rise.

"You don't think they'll try to kidnap us again, do you?" I can't hide my worry with the words, and burrow under Patrick's arm.

"Let them try." Auntie's tone is calm. "There have been many who've tried to find us here, and none have ever succeeded. You are under our protection now, and you are safe at Zanetti."

Twenty

MERRY

The second full day at Zanetti proves that the people are every bit as good as we initially thought. Now that our story is known, people don't only greet us, they stop and tell us that they support our work, support us in trying to rescue the captive women. Each and every one brings a tear to my eyes, and I fully blame the pregnancy hormones. After our fourth hug of the morning, the emotions are starting to get to me. No one has treated us differently because of our political positions, and frankly, no one seems to care. Auntie has the ultimate say-so here, and everyone is secure in her leadership.

The men are off lending a hand with a wall repair—with Glitch moaning the entire way about the lack of instantaneous response to his trap; Mav is off in the airport, working on repairs for some of Zanetti's vehicles; and Nell and I were invited to a women's circle. I'm not entirely certain what that entails, except that there will be women present. Nell, as per usual, chatters happily to Sheena, who is escorting us to the circle, while I'm lost in thought. Anxiety nips at my heels about the upcoming missions, along with worry over what we'll do if the person we're looking for doesn't take the

169

bait. How will we find them? We can hunt down the trust, but that could genuinely just be an environmentally conscious donor. If neither pan out, we're back to zero. I do *not* want to be back at zero. Because the king isn't going to keep waiting, he's going to dismantle the so-called EICs, and whoever was responsible will be in the wind.

We arrive at our destination, and I'm surprised to see women and girls gathered around large kitchen worktables, and huge pots boiling along one wall. Rather than a normal stove, they have created an entire wall of cooking surface, and the steaming pots are lined up tidily in a row. Women are cutting chunks off of colored ropes on the work tops, while the children run to various cut piles and pass the colorful chunks to one woman, who appears to be in charge, and who then tosses them into one pot or another.

I stop inside the doorway, confused. Nell doesn't bat an eye, just walks to the nearest opening along the way, and someone hands her a knife. She starts chopping, and never stops talking. For a woman with a troubled past, she has never had a problem fitting in. Yet here I am, balanced just outside of the action. My right hand falls to my belly, a habit I'm finding more and more automatic these days. As I look around for some clue of what's going on, another woman bustles into the room with a roll cart piled high with white fabric. I watch her buzz by in curiosity.

"People in doorways are racked with indecision, and that's no way to lead, Mrs. Royce." Auntie's ever-calm tone startles me from my spot leaned in the doorjamb.

"Hi, Auntie. Sorry, I just . . . was trying to figure out what was going on." I fiddle with the end of my braid nervously. Her mild rebuke makes me nervous, even though we've recently met. She radiates wisdom, and I find myself hoping for her approval.

170

"Ahh, my dear." She settles one wrinkled hand on my shoulder affectionately. "We can never know it all. Look at your friend, there. See how she jumps in with both feet?"

I nod, and she continues, "She lives with the vigor of one who's been released from a cage. Yet here you hover as if you're scared to walk into one." Her eyes bore into me, and it feels like she sees more than I'm ready to share.

"I, well . . ."

"You don't have to explain yourself, dearie. But I want you to think on this: Living in *fear* of the cage, is just putting yourself into it for them." Her brows draw down, and she purses her lips in consternation. "That's no way to live. You must walk in abundance, in confidence, and in friendship. You will do great things for this world; I can sense it. But first, you must believe it. And whatever has shaken you, you must cast it aside. For to lead others, you must first lead yourself."

Her words settle on my shoulders like a warm blanket in a cold wind. "Thank you, Auntie. It feels like I'll never be as good at this as you are. Were you always a natural leader?"

Her booming laugh startles me and draws every eye in the room to us. "My girl, no! I was a skinny waif with braids on my head and a fire in my belly. Nothing more, nothing less. But time shapes us to its own will, and this is where it has led me." She pats my shoulder in reassurance. "Now, no more heaviness. Today is a day for companionship, and your Nell has the right of it. We're dyeing today, and we've got much to do—so your extra hands will be appreciated."

Oh, dye! I look around the room at the rainbow of beautiful linens adorning the women, and smile. *This is going to be fun.*

Many hours later, Sheena leads Nell and me—exhausted beyond belief, and covered in specks of dye—back to our rooms. She seems to have come out of her shell after spending the day with Nell, and the three of us discuss the various dye techniques favored by the many opinionated women we worked with today. Thanks to our efforts, we were generously gifted with skirts for ourselves, as well as decorative tunics for both of our husbands. At least we'll have something for tomorrow . . . Apparently in all of our running and moving and plotting, we've all forgotten the time passing—but it's Christmas Eve today.

Despite our growing independence here, the tunnels all look the same, and we need help to get anywhere off of our own hallway. Luckily, the people have been happy to help us. Warmth for these people has grown in me so quickly, it's shocking. With the Resistance, I was skeptical—and frankly judgmental—of their lifestyle. I was able to overcome my preconceptions, to see the *people* in time. But here, it's an entirely different story.

I'm as far away from my home in Jackson Flats as I can be—we're underground, on the other side of the continent, buried under countless feet of rock and snow, and yet the warmth and comfort of home surrounds me. It's the magic of Zanetti.

Once I'm back in my room, I quickly squirrel away Patrick's tunic, so I can surprise him tomorrow morning. Walking out of the bedroom, I freeze when I see Sheena waiting nervously by our small dining table. "Hi, Sheena. I thought you'd already be on your way home. Is everything okay?"

"Oh, uhm, yes! Everything is fine, it's just . . . well, are you pregnant? I thought you might be, and it's okay if you're not." She blushes. "We have a tradition here, that the first person to notice the pregnancy gives a gift, and a blessing. So, we all like to guess, and I noticed you kept putting your hand on your stomach earlier, so . . ." She trails off, looking both embarrassed and curious.

I give her a small smile of encouragement. "You're right, I am. I'm not far along yet, and with everything going on we haven't really told anyone." My smile turns into forlorn sadness. *My own family doesn't even know.*

"Oh, I understand. Well, I won't tell anyone else. But, I do want you to have something, and a blessing for the wee one to come." She addresses my stomach as she continues, "Whether the sun shines or the snowstorm rages, may the light of your soul always guide you." She bows low, and then from behind her back she pulls out the tiniest little gown I've ever seen. It's intricately stitched around the neck, and gathered up at the hem, with an opening left for easy diaper changing. The design is a kaleidoscope of colors, using almost every color we made today. She must have worked on it all day, and now she's giving it to me, someone she's only known for two days. Tears build in my eyes, and I frantically try to blink them away, to no avail.

"Do you like it?" she asks hopefully.

I sniffle, and without thinking throw my arms around her, and sob into her shoulder. "I'm so sorry, it's - just . . . so . . . *nice.*" The sobs wrack my body, and it crosses my mind briefly to be embarrassed at crying all over a new acquaintance, but she takes it in stride.

Sheena shushes me and hugs me back for a few moments, until a familiar warmth reaches my side, and takes over. Patrick's soothing voice and masculine smell hit me at once, and I cling to his shirt like he's going to vanish. In time, the tears slow, and I continue clinging to him. He carries me over to our stone bench and settles me in his lap.

"Are you okay?" he asks, once the hiccupping sobs have fully subsided.

I nod, unable to speak yet.

"Do you want to talk about it?"

Do I want to talk about it? Where to even begin? Rather than answer, I shove the tiny, beautiful gown at him.

He takes it from my hands delicately and admires it with a soft smile on his handsome face. "I think I understand."

I search his eyes, wondering if he can understand the depth of emotion I'm feeling right now. He strokes my cheek so gently and looks at me like I'm the most beautiful thing he's ever seen. *That can't be right—I'm all red and blotchy.*

"This is the first of many beautiful, thoughtful gifts our baby is going to receive. It makes it so real, doesn't it?" I nod and reach out to gently trace one of the bright streaks of turquoise running the length of the gown. "I can only imagine how hard it has been to be away from your family for so many months, and now with a baby on the way, we both want to be back home with them, to share this special time with them. But we're so *close*, Sadie, I promise. Come hell or high water, I will wade through it to get you back where you belong. And I'll be by your side because that's where I belong."

I smile tilts the corner of his mouth, and I sigh. "I love you." Those are the only words I can say in the moment. They're so small, but encompass such a huge feeling I have for this man, who's become my rock so quickly amidst this storm we're in. He stands and carries me to yet another temporary bed. We've had far too many, in this short marriage so far. But there's one thing I know now that I didn't before. Home isn't a single spot in Jackson Flats.

It isn't baked into the sun-drenched fields I worked and loved my entire childhood. It isn't even a fireplace with my family gathered around it at Christmas time, laughing and sharing mama's amazing cocoa, though that is part of it.

Home is where your heart leads you, where it clings fast, and where it finds the one your soul loves.

TWENTY-ONE

MOUSE, MEET CHEESE

Christmas begins in a blur of food and fun, but still, I miss home. It's my first Christmas ever away from my family back in Georada, and I wonder how Peter's doing with his injuries, how Teddy and Faith are doing with the pregnancy, and I miss every single one of my family members. Patrick promises me that next year we'll be home, and I hope he's able to keep that promise. The five of us are sitting around in a small entertainment room off our hallway, with sofas and a decorative mantel. There are no fireplaces or trees here, but they've still made it festive with bright swags of linens, and small twinkly lights.

There's a natural lull in the conversation, and I'm leaning against Patrick's arm, feeling dozy in the warm, quiet room. My eyelids begin to flutter when a rapid *beep-beep-beep* emits from Glitch's watch. He sits bolt upright and taps it to review the alert.

"Guys! They took the bait! We got a response." He falls silent for a moment, reading.

My sleepy, cozy moment is forgotten, and we all sit forward to hear what they said in return.

"They want to meet me, tomorrow at seven p.m. They sent an address right outside of Wrightsville—only one town over. Let's see, let's see . . ." He talks to himself as he quickly extracts his tablet from his messenger bag, and looks up the address.

My heart is pounding, and it's suddenly very, very real that we are close to the end of this. *Please, please let this be the end of this.*

"The town has been primarily closed, including this coffee shop. It looks like there's a single operating waystation, due to proximity to the capital. This is good, I think. Right?" He looks up, and scrunches his mouth to the side, clearly uncertain.

"It sounds about right, to me," Atlas agrees. "We suspect someone close to your father, so it makes sense to be near the capital. A closed city also makes sense, because there's a lower chance of witnesses. The only real question is if we can get there in time and provide sufficient surveillance coverage." He taps his knee idly, thinking it over.

"Time to call Mav, then," I suggest.

"Agreed, I'll run and get her," Patrick offers, giving me a quick squeeze around the waist before he heads for the door.

"Did they sign it in any way, or is there any information you can get from the email address about who it is?"

Glitch sighs. "It's a randomized account, generated from within the king's server. While eventually I might be able to get some scrap of information, this person is clearly well-connected. If they want to cover their tracks, it would be easy to access someone else's comm station in the office to send this."

"So, we wait. At least we have something to prepare for, now." Nell shrugs one shoulder, indifferent.

A few minutes later, Patrick and Mav re-enter the room. Glitch quickly fills her in on the location, and Atlas runs down a list from memory of the equipment he'll need to pick up from his nearest storage warehouse on the way.

Mav rubs her hands together in gleeful anticipation. "A'right, a'right, a'right! Let's do this thang. I can be ready in three hours. Can you five get your things and say your good-byes 'fore then?"

We look around the room, all nodding assent. One after the other, we rise and head towards the hallway, to pack up our few belongings and supplies. Atlas puts his arm out to stop me in the doorway. "Sadie, let's not forget your trip to the med room. We'll need Glitch's evidence packed to go."

I sigh, dreading it even though it was my idea. "I know."

Mav grins. "Come on, I'll take you."

We walk through the twisting tunnels, taking yet another branch I haven't seen yet. I run my hand along the gentle warmth of the stone wall next to me, and a pang of sadness hits that it's likely to be my last day at Zanetti. For all its wonders and strangeness, it has been a true sanctuary to our little band of refugees. Mav stops abruptly and holds a door open for me to enter. Unlike the rest of the mountain, there is a nip in the air, and the lights are harsh overhead.

I huff out a breath. *No matter where you are, medical facilities don't change much.* A woman in a brightly colored sarong dress waits next to an elevated stone table.

"Hello, Sadie. Please lie back right here, and we'll get you taken care of." Her smile is kind, but nerves get the better of me.

"Should I be worried that you want to put me on a stone table, and we're this close to a volcano? You're not planning to pull a switcheroo, and sacrifice me, are you?" I joke.

Mav snorts, "Word on the street is, you no longer meet the criteria, wit' a bun in the oven."

I'm so shocked by her retort that I let out a great belly laugh and forget to be nervous. The brightly adorned doctor is quick and efficient, but I stop her before she pulls the needle from my arm.

"What is it, ma'am?" She looks concerned.

"Do you have a genetic study program here?"

"Yes, but I assure you that your entire sample leaves with you. We do *not* perform tests without consent."

I give her a nod. "Good. Take another vial please." I close my eyes quickly, so I don't have to see the blood.

She does what I ask, then removes the needle from my arm. Capping the samples, she hands me two vials of my blood, and holds a third empty one. Begrudgingly, I reach up and snatch a few strands from the back of my head before passing them to her to stick into the third vial. She swirls them into a tidy knot, and then tucks them inside and seals it, too.

Once it's done, she passes me the vial, and gives a short bow. Before she turns away, I stop her with a hand on her arm.

"Here." I extend one of the vials of blood, and her eyes go round.

"Sadie, Mrs. Royce, ah . . ." She looks to Mav in confusion, who shrugs, and continues watching the exchange with raised brows. "You don't have to do that."

"I know I don't have to, and that's why I am. The people who aren't hungry for power are those who will use it wisely. I hope this helps your genetics program, and please contact us if I can help in any other way in the future." I press the vial firmly into her palm, and she finally takes it.

"This will mean so much for the future of Zanetti, and The People thank you." This time, her bow is low, and the tied top of her sarong nearly brushes the floor.

"It is the least we can do, given your kindness and hospitality. Back home, I'd have made you all dinner. For now, well . . . I suppose that will have to do."

She looks with wonder at what she holds, and her words are reverent. "You have more than paid us in kind for simple aid, which we would have provided you freely."

"Good, I'm glad you will accept my offer." Swinging my legs around, I slowly rise from the stone table. My head spins, and I sway for a moment. *I hate blood draws. I'd make a terrible lab rat.*

Mav reaches out a hand to steady me, and I gratefully accept it as I slide from the table to the floor. We slowly walk out, and about halfway back to our rooms the world steadies. I tentatively release Mav's arm. She stuffs her hands into her bomber jacket's pockets.

"I don't know how you can wear that thing down here, Mav. It's too hot for real clothes," I observe idly.

She snorts. "This hea' is my armor. Wear it all the time, no matter the weather."

My thoughts drift back to the day I put on my favorite jeans to leave Georada—jeans long since left behind in Mairmont—and I know exactly what she means.

"That was real' generous of you, Sadie," she continues.

I wave her off, not wanting to talk about it.

"Right when I think I understand you, you go changin' on me again." She shakes her head, and I'm left to ponder what she means by that as we walk the last few feet of the hall until she drops me off at our room. We part with a silent wave, and I enter to find Patrick already zipping up a duffel bag with our meager possessions.

"All done?" he asks.

"Yep, I'm just a bit lighter." I hold up the two vials and give them a small shake to illustrate.

He nods and—in trade for our vials of proof—hands me a piece of the delicious crusty bread already slathered with tangy butter. Musk-ox butter, as it turns out.

I chew happily, my feet up on our stone bench as I watch him make one last circuit of the room, checking for anything we'd left behind. Satisfied that there is nothing left, he throws the light bag over his shoulder, and stands in front of me. "Ready to head out?"

With a nod, I hold up a hand for him to pull me up. I'm once again tired, since my earlier nap got disrupted by Glitch's big news. He hauls me to my feet, and my body brushes against his. The brief contact sends a frisson of heat through me, and I sway for a second. He steadies me with his left hand, and then sets the bag down on our dining table. He plucks the last few bites of bread from my hand, and sets it next to the bag.

"Hey! I wasn't done with that yet—" I try to argue, but he silences me with a sweltering kiss. From zero to molten in two-point-five seconds flat.

His hands thread into my hair, and I lean to the side to give him better access. My heart is beating wildly against my ribcage, and where my hand rests on his chest, I feel his beating every bit as fast. The kiss is a sweet eternity, and when he releases me, I sigh at his absence. He runs the back of his knuckles from my temple, slowly down my jaw and to the corner of my well-kissed lips.

"I love you so much, and I can't wait to get to the next chapter of our lives together. Where we can settle down, find a home, and raise this baby together," he whispers. "We're almost done, Sadie. I can feel it in my bones." He rests his forehead against mine, and for

181

a moment we're frozen, breathing the same air, reveling in being together.

"I love you too, Patrick," I whisper in return, and lean up to plant a soft return kiss on his forehead. Trailing kisses down his face on the same path he traced on my own, I land back on his lips. The kiss is tender, and full of promise.

We may not have many worldly possessions, but I'd trade it all again in a heartbeat for another day with this man. Hand in hand, we left our room, and headed back to the underground airport to leave Zanetti for good. *For you must leave your knowledge of Zanetti behind you when you go.*

We have to fly through the night and, unlike the trip to Alaska Territories, I find myself restless and unable to sleep on the way to Wrightsville. All the possible outcomes of the next twenty-four hours play on loop in my brain, and I desperately wish for a way to shut them off. Patrick's soft snores in the window seat meld with the hum of the plane's engines, and eventually I drift to fitful sleep.

A crack of lightning in the night sky wakes me an indeterminate time later, and I sit upright with a jolt. Looking around, I see Atlas standing directly outside the cockpit, discussing something with Mav. He nods at something I can't hear and returns to his seat in the row ahead of ours.

"Everything okay?" I whisper, not wanting to wake Patrick or Nell, both sleeping through the natural commotion.

"She says we're at the very edge of the storm, so we don't need to land. She's already adjusted our flight pattern to accommodate."

Thank God for Mav's wicked flight skills.

He rolls his shoulders, and settles back into the seat, but doesn't close his eyes. Staring out the window, I can tell he's having the same problem I am with sleeplessness. We sit in silence for some time when he surprises me by speaking again.

"I'm worried about Glitch. He's putting a lot on his shoulders, and I can tell he feels personally responsible for the success of this mission." He pauses, and his jaw twitches as if in indecision, something I never pegged Atlas to struggle with. "You . . . you're pretty good with people. Maybe when we land, you can remind him that we've got his back. And that it's not on him alone. I think he'll listen to you."

Having said his piece, he crosses his arms over his broadly muscled chest, and slouches down to rest his head against the back of his seat before closing his eyes.

Taking his example, I lean back against Patrick's arm, and shut my eyes once again.

The morning dawns cold and gray, with snow clouds gathering overhead in the small city of Juniper. For a place a stone's throw from the capital, it's truly a ghost town. Proximity has earned it better preservation than most, however, and the town has an eerie feel to it as a result. It's almost as if it's holding its breath, waiting for all of its missing residents to walk in and open it back up later this afternoon. Instead, it's sat here sealed and abandoned and will continue to sit for the foreseeable future. *Maybe forever if the*

population doesn't start increasing again soon. The dismal thought matches the gloomy day.

I stamp my feet to ward off the cold, watching as Atlas ducks into a third building, searching for the perfect place to wait out our trap. *Hopefully he finds a place with working heat.*

A moment later, he pops his head back out and waves us all in. Glitch lets out a throaty sigh, and starts toward the door. Atlas's request last night surfaces, and I call out, "Hey, Glitch?"

He turns, and after I wave Patrick and Nell inside, we're alone in the desolate street. "What's up, Sadie-cup?"

I shake my head at his half-hearted attempt at banter, and give him a crooked smile. "Your expectations, I think."

He looks confused. "What?"

"I just want to make sure that you know we're all behind you on this. You're the one going in there, but we're all responsible for how things go today. You know that, right?" I reach out and give his hand a squeeze, the effect somewhat muffled by our gloves.

He looks down and shuffles his feet. "I know that, but . . ." He trails off.

"It's hard to *believe* that. But I'm serious, Glitch. We're all behind you, and we all came to this plan together. Whatever happens in there today, we'll deal with it together, too."

He nods, and meets my eyes with a grateful expression. Pushing his glasses up his nose, he still seems nervous. "Thanks, Sadie."

I give him one final pat on the shoulder as we walk into our mission headquarters.

TWENTY-TWO

SPLAT

Glitch is nervous. He's normally a little spastic, but right now he's in overdrive. He's fiddled with the strap on his bag, the pin camera hidden there, his glasses, the two vials inside the bag, his tablet, his recording pen, his pepper spray, his taser, the body cam, and—most worrisome—the earpiece in his ear. Unable to take it a second longer, I walk over, and grab both of his hands mid-fiddle with the neck of his shirt. He's back in standard-issue Resistance fatigues, just in case.

"Glitch, for the love of all that's holy and Mama's buttermilk biscuits, hold *still*," I urge him.

He blushes. "Sorry, Sadie. I want to make sure I don't forget anything. I mean, there's a lot riding on this. If one of the cameras doesn't pick up, or if I say the wrong thing, or—I mean, this would be the absolute worst—but, what if nobody shows at all?" He swallows hard, Adam's apple bobbing with the motion.

"Then we'll figure it out. That's the only option." Slowly, like I'm dealing with a spooky colt, I release his hands. He clenches them into fists and holds them down by his sides.

Better, but not by a whole lot. "It's almost time. Are you sure you want to do this? It doesn't have to be you. I'll go, or Atlas can go."

Atlas nods his agreement, arms crossed and face impassive, his usual stance during operations.

"No, no, no. We've been over this. It has to be me. Too immature"—he points at Nell—"too unbelievable"—Patrick—"too pregnant and therefore not-risk-able"—me—"and too intimidating"—Atlas.

"Nonetheless, the offer still stands," I insist.

He takes a deep breath and seems to find his calm. "Thank you, Sadie. But I can do this." His eyes are steady, so I step back with a nod.

"Go get 'em, Glitch," Mav says from her place propped in a corner chair. Her eyes are still closed, after a long night of flying and then hiding our plane before our backup arrived. The NAA Police are stationed in hiding at key points around the city, and once Glitch and the mystery man are inside, they'll surround the place. The king was more than happy to send his best men to see this done with.

"You've got this, my man." Patrick walks over, and extends a hand to shake.

Glitch grips it in return. "Thanks, Rick-raff."

Nell and Atlas also offer encouragement as he walks towards the door, and then he's gone. We all settle in behind the monitor bank and watch through the various cameras hidden on his person as he walks down the street, to a bank across the street from the coffee shop where the meeting is supposed to happen. Slipping inside, he settles into a chair he'd placed there earlier.

For nearly an hour, we all wait in silence. Nell's crunching on various snacks is the only sound. To my surprise, Glitch doesn't fidget. He sits stock still in the chair, hands fastened into its poofy paisley fabric armrests like his life depends on it.

Then, a familiar silver hover vehicle pulls past the building and continues on down the street. We catch it on the cameras a few times, and it seems like the driver is doing a patrol of the small city in advance. The dark tint means we can't catch a glimpse yet of who's inside. The suspense is killing me. Eventually satisfied, the sleek vehicle pulls to a stop on the opposite side of the coffee shop. We hear a distant snap of door hinges opening, and then a clunk of the door shutting again. After that, all is quiet. Glitch waits five more minutes, as Atlas instructed, before rising slowly from the chair, and exiting the bank. It feels as though we're right there with him, given our view and the motion from the various body cameras. He slips into the front door of the coffee shop, and the back of a woman in a sharp suit comes into view. Her hair is in a tightly-bound twist on the back of her head, and her pumps are rather more serviceable than showy. A nervous energy fills the room, and even Mav has given up her comfy chair in favor of being upright, and watching over our shoulders.

"I wasn't sure you'd come," Glitch opens without a single waiver in his voice. My heart soars at his bravery.

A bored female voice drifts over her shoulder, and she doesn't turn immediately. "Yes, well, you have something I want. Or so you say."

Patrick freezes stiff to my right, and I hastily look over to see why, and after taking in his horrified face, I turn back to the screen.

She turns slowly, deliberately taking her time and not looking the least bit concerned. "Are you prepared to prove yourself, Mr. . . . Glitch, is it?"

Good gracious, it's Patrick's mother.

He nods in response.

"What an odd name." She pauses again, waiting. When he doesn't move fast enough to suit her, she snaps her fingers impatiently. "Are you going to show me, or keep standing there like an idiot? I haven't got all day!"

Glitch fumbles a bit opening the messenger back, and jostles one of the cameras along the strap. One of our monitors goes a hair sideways but doesn't stop recording. The vials clank together softly as he holds them aloft, but doesn't move any closer.

With an annoyed sigh, she strides across the room. At the last second, he steps back, holding the vials behind his back. "Why? I want to know why you were willing to betray your own husband, first," he demands.

She laughs, the sound cold in the empty space. "Your mistake is in thinking I betrayed him *first*. He failed me long ago. Now, hand those over so I can test them."

Stunned by her lack of remorse, I look back at Patrick and see true chagrin on his face, his head now propped by his elbows on the arms of the chair as he helplessly watches the scene unfold. I snake an arm between his bicep and forearm and rest a supportive hand on the muscle corded there.

Glitch silently hands the vials to Queen Deb, who inserts them into a small, square machine pulled from her suit pocket. It hums for sixty seconds, and then lights up green.

"Match found—let's verify." She presses a button, and something flashes on the screen that only she can see. "Well, well. A silly name, but not an unfounded threat. Richardson was wrong about you after all." She slips the vials out of the machine, and into her suit pocket.

"What do you want in exchange for the girl?" she asks in a bored tone.

"Only the girl?" Glitch rapid-fires back.

She rolls her eyes, and props a hand on her hip, bunching her suit jacket in the process. "Yes, *only* the girl. I'd rather my dear son not know I'm involved. I'm sure you'll tell him, but he won't believe you. Now, stop beating around the bush. How much?" she snaps.

"I'm afraid you won't be getting what you want, after all," Glitch says, the first hint of disgust creeping into his voice.

"Trust me, we will. Give me a price, and it will be deposited in the account of your choice within ninety seconds." She taps her ear confidently, indicating that someone is listening in for the account number.

"There's just one problem with that. I don't put a price on people." The doors at either end of the coffee shop blow inward simultaneously, and Deb screams, covering her head as splinters fly. Glitch steps back, and uniformed members of the NAA Police swoop her up under both arms before she has a chance to try and run. The testing machine flies from her hands and bounces with a thud off of the nearest wall.

They turn and carry her towards the door, but Glitch shouts for them to stop. Jogging over, he pats Deb's sides until he finds the pocket with the vials, and extracts them. He jiggles them before her face one last time, before returning them to his messenger bag. "Go ahead." He nods, and as the police carry her out she screams threats towards Glitch over her shoulder the entire way.

We pile out of the temporary headquarters, and rush to meet Glitch at the coffee shop. The rest of our group rushes in, but I stop, dragging Patrick to a halt with me. "Are you okay?" I search his face for signs of how he's feeling, but he's got his emotions under tight lock and key.

"Not at all." He runs a hand through his hair. "But it's not about me, right now. Let's see this through, and deal with the fallout later." He spins on his heel, and storms into the coffee shop, leaving me stunned in his wake.

TWENTY-THREE

MOMMY DEAREST

I take a swig of cocoa from the paper cup Nell passes me, but wince in revulsion. It tastes like cardboard water with a sadly mistreated cocoa bean in it. Shuddering, I pass it back. I'd rather be thirsty than drink that. She takes a swig, and shrugs. "Tastes fine to me."

"Your standards are lower than the baby's," I whisper accusingly. We're relatively secluded in this hallway, but there are police all over the place in this station and I don't want to risk being overheard. Patrick, Glitch, and Atlas are giving a lengthy report in one of the rooms, but Nell and I are spared the interrogation for now. I'm sure our time is coming, but for the time being we're relegated to the hallway, and piss-poor hot cocoa pilfered from the break room.

I'm staring at the toes of my borrowed black winter boots, when footsteps echo down the long hallway. I don't bother looking up, since quite a few cops have traipsed by to check out the circus act that is our reappearance. This time, however, the footsteps stop a few feet away. Nell elbows me in the ribs, and I swat at her hand.

Finally looking up, I gasp and leap to my feet. "Peter!" I fling myself into his waiting arms, and nearly bowl him right into the wall.

He laughs, and squeezes me tight. "I missed you too, Sadie-bear. I missed you too." He lifts my feet off the ground, and spins me in a circle.

I laugh, feeling like a kid again for just a minute. When my feet touch the ground again, I stagger back a step. He grabs my arms to steady me, and chuckles. Growing serious, he gives me his sternest older-brother voice. "I am not *ever* letting you out of my sight again, young lady. I about had a heart attack, waking up on the side of that cursed road, finding you two gone." He adjusts his arm in the sling where it's still tied close to his body with a grimace.

Whoops, a little too rough with him still on the mend.

"It wasn't like we had a choice, Peter. We were kidnapped, not joyriding."

"I know, and it killed me every dang day." His voice is tight, and the guilt permeating the small hallway is suffocating.

"Hey, it was *not* your fault. You know that, right? Peter?" I demand, but he dodges my gaze, looking stubbornly over my shoulder.

"I was in charge of your safety, and you were snatched. On my watch, with me feet away. You could have been killed, or worse. I'll never forgive myself." His voice is hollow now, and the joy of the moment is sucked away that fast.

"Peter, that's ridiculous. There were so many of them, and only one of you. Nobody blames—"

The interview room door slams open, and Patrick storms out. He halts abruptly, taking in my upset mood, and Peter's miserable face.

"Patrick," Peter says with a nod.

"Peter, good to see you," Patrick returns.

"Anything I can help with?" Peter asks, back in professional mode.

Patrick runs an angry hand through his very mussed hair. "I have no clue. They brought Mom in, but she won't talk. Other than the one slip about Richardson with Glitch, she's been completely mum about who he is or who else she's been working with, or why. She's demanding to be released, and stating she was 'merely acting to get the princess returned.' They want me to go in, and see if she'll slip up, but I . . . can't. Not right this minute."

"Let's get a cup of coffee," Peter says, tone mild. "Ladies, we'll be back in a bit."

I hate seeing Patrick so torn up about this, and can only imagine how the king must be feeling at the news of the betrayal. Resolved, I march to the interview room door, and let myself in. Glitch and Atlas are arguing with the NAA police captain of Wrightsville, but they all fall silent when the door clicks shut behind me.

"I'll do it. I'll talk to her," I blurt, not wasting any time. *I need to get in there before Patrick gets back.*

"Sadie, I don't think it's going to help. She's not talking to anyone," Atlas mutters.

"It can't hurt. Can it?" I turn to the police captain, and stand firm.

He shrugs, not caring one way or the other. "We need someone with a personal connection. You two haven't met, but maybe she'll leak something. If not, we can always try again with the prince."

"Then let's do it, right now," I urge, and he stands. "Oh, wait. Glitch, I need your video player."

His brow crinkles in confusion. "What, why?"

"Just a hunch." I wiggle my fingers, and he reluctantly places it in my palm. Ready, I turn and follow the captain to the other end of the hall, around a few corners, past a set of armed guards, and into a room surrounded by floor-to-ceiling windows. The queen sits in the middle, looking bored as she examines her nails at the bare white table. The captain speaks to the guards briefly, and then swings the door open barely wide enough for me to slip through.

Once I'm in, the walls look black, belying the fact that we're being watched from every angle. Deb looks up, and raises her eyebrows in surprise. "Well, my, my. I did not expect to see you in here," she muses.

"Oh? Why not?" I settle into the chair across the table from her, working to keep my face neutral.

Sarcasm drips from her tone as she says, "There's quite a rumor going around that you've been kidnapped."

"Ahh, well. That's actually not a rumor. We were kidnapped. I hear you were trying very hard to get me back. Thanks for that, I guess." I tap my nails lightly on the tabletop a few times, thinking over the best approach.

She snorts with indignation. "Cut the crap. I know they sent you in here to get something out of me, but it's not going to work. You can march your skinny butt right back out the door because you're wasting your time. I want to speak to my husband."

"Ooh, I can't imagine he wants to speak to you right now. After you said he was a failure? No, wait. What was it you said? You betrayed him because he betrayed you first?" I tsked disapprovingly. "Somehow, I think yours is worse. Just a guess, though. I don't know what he did, after all." I give her my brightest smile and tip my head to the side.

Her eyes narrow, and I can see her turning it over, trying to figure out my angle.

"Besides, I don't really care what you two did or didn't do to each other. That's not my concern—besides, a lot of people these days hate their spouses. I can imagine it's even harder to stay happy with all the political pressure you two are under. The spotlight. People judging you at every turn." I tap the table twice, hard, to draw her attention. "What I want to know is, how could you turn against other women like that? That's what I find so hard to understand."

She rolls her eyes at me, and I consider telling her they'll get stuck like that. Not the point. "I'm sure this is hard for a small-town girl like yourself to understand," she says, voice thick with condescension, "but throwing you under the bus doesn't give me heartburn. If it gets me to my end goals, I couldn't care less about one woman, even if you are married to my son." She leans forward, her gaze acidic as she looks me up and down. "Your genes may be special, but nothing else about you is. He'll be better off once you're out of the picture, and he's married to someone more appropriate."

"I'm sorry you feel that way, I was hoping we'd get along one day, being we're family now. But, I'll live." I shake my head. "No, it's not me that I'm wondering about. I want to know how you were so willing to turn on all the *other* women?"

She glares at the nearest camera mounted in the corner and speaks directly into it. "Could you please get her out of here? She's delusional." When no response is forthcoming, she levels a bored gaze back on me. "It's worse than I thought. Apparently, you don't even know what's special about yourself. You're the only one. There isn't anyone else *alive* with the same genetic makeup as you. Now. Get me my husband." She demands, but I ignore her. Thankfully, so do the officers waiting outside.

"No, I don't think I will, because you still haven't answered my question. I want to know how you could turn on the rest of the women. You seem confused, though. Allow me to jog your memory."

Tapping Glitch's video player in the way I've seen him do it so many times, I start the video of our rescue mission, right at the point where we burst through the doorway, and then come into the room filled with sedated women. As it zooms in on the individual faces of each woman in turn, shock crosses her features briefly before she locks it down. On the last face, I pause the screen.

"You didn't know about them, did you?"

She leans back in her chair, refusing to speak.

"I'll tell you about them. That woman there? That's Paige. She's currently in a medically-induced coma, caused by the sedation drugs that have been pumped into her around the clock for *seven years*. Seven years, strapped to a bed, your life going by without you. Impregnated, repeatedly, forced to give birth and the babies taken, one after the other. All while you slept."

The color slowly drains from Deb's face as I talk, and my hunch is confirmed. *It wasn't her.* I lean forward, going in for the kill.

"You see, Deb, it's not me you're on trial for. Because I'm right here, fine as can be." I wiggle my fingers in a flagrant wave. "But Paige, she's not. She's still in testing, undergoing treatment after treatment to try to wake her, so she can meet her seventh child. Because she just gave birth, by cesarean, to her seventh child. A little girl, with curly black hair and green eyes. She looks like a little cherub, truly. And as far as I can tell, she's never been awake to hold a single one of her babies." I let that awful truth sink in for a moment.

"Someone out there is using women like breeding cattle, Deb. And right now, everybody in this building thinks it's you, except me."

Her eyes snap to mine, and I can see that she's finally caught up to where this is going.

"The thing is, I don't particularly like you. So, seeing you go to jail doesn't bother me all that much. However, I do like your son a whole heck of a lot. Love him, actually. And watching you go to jail would tear him to shreds, which I'm not okay with. So, here's what I think needs to happen—you need to give up Richardson, whoever he is. You don't have the stomach for what he's got planned, and what he's been doing. I can tell, based on your reaction to this video." I tap to rewind it, and press play again.

She averts her eyes, and I know I've struck home. "There aren't just four, either. This was one *small* facility. There is one of these in every single tri-state. Some of them hold more than fifteen women. You can do the math on that because I know you're calculating." I can't resist the jab, though it's not to the point.

I lean back, and this time I'm the one examining my nails. I wait, and after a long moment of her continued silence, I sigh and stand. "Well, I tried. At least I can go tell Patrick that I said my piece, and he'll appreciate the effort to save his mother, though I'm not sure you're worth saving, frankly. Anyone who lets the person really responsible for this go free, well, you deserve to go to jail, too." I turn and slowly head for the door.

I twist the knob, and she blurts out, "Wait!"

Without a care in the world, I turn back to face her, remaining silent. *I've talked enough to last me a week.*

197

"You're right, I didn't know what he was doing to those women. He told me he needed you, due to your unique genes. We discussed at length how unsuitable you were for a royal appointment, and decided it would be best to remove you from the picture early on, so Patrick could be re-matched. He said that studying you would be what the NAA needed to become the world leader, and turn our population rates around in under two years. He promised me that it would be better for everyone, and that we'd rule together." She swallows hard, struggling to continue.

"And, who is he?" I prod, scared to dry up the flow of words she's finally saying.

"Brody. Brody Richardson, of Satellite Security." The defeat in her tone is thick enough to cut with a knife.

"I've never heard of Satellite Security. Have you got a photo of him?"

She inclines her head. "On my phone. I'll unlock it, if someone brings it in." She glances back up at the camera before staring back at her lap. "Surely Patrick must know I'd never be involved in something that *heinous*," she says to me, while we wait for the phone to be brought in.

I don't respond, having had more than my fill of her self-righteousness. Peter is the one to bring the phone in, so I know that Patrick is outside, and my heart hurts for him. Even if his mother isn't the one behind the evil taking place at the Environmental Impact Centers, his family will be torn apart by this. Peter places the phone in the middle of the table, and then turns and exits without a word. Deb leans forward, and the phone scans her face before unlocking.

"Show me Brody," she commands, and a photo loads instantly. She shoves the device across the table to me, and my jaw drops in shock.

Twenty-Four

APPARENT

Three Days Later

The hum of the airplane's engines abruptly cuts off, and my heart jumps into my throat. I glance over at Patrick, and his calm smile woos me back into the moment. Focus, focus. Mav exits the cockpit without any fanfare—as is her way—and gives us a saucy wink.

"Y'all don't be faintin' on me now, this is 'bout to get good." She drops the door open in a rush, and takes the steps down two at a time. Patrick follows behind her at a steadier pace, and I follow a heartbeat behind him. Nell and Atlas are right behind us. Glitch chose to stay back in Wrightsville, given his part in things.

A nondescript black transport truck awaits us on the grassy air strip, and I climb into the back, suppressing a huff. *This is the last time, Sadie. Suck it up.*

The ride is quick, and before I know it we're pulling through the high gates of the Resistance compound. Everything looks so different to me now than it did before, and I find myself going back down some of the happier memories here, of people who are different than me, but accepting. We roll to a stop directly next to the gathering field, and it is packed. People cover every square inch of grass, and butterflies swarm my stomach at the thought of standing up in front of them all.

The back doors swing wide, and Patrick stands, extending me a hand. "Shall we, Princess Sadie?"

He uses my formal title as a reminder, and I square my shoulders. Taking his hand, we walk out of the back of the transport with our heads held high. Even in black fatigues, I can feel the power in our walk, and I revel in the moment.

The crowd parts, and we make a beeline directly for the stage, where Brock and the remaining leaders of the Resistance wait. People clap as we walk by, happy to see us returned safely to the flock. Brock claps as we approach, but in his eyes I see reproach, not welcome. Turning towards the assembled crowd, I spot Pierce in the front row, looking very unhappy at our return. My heart squeezes at the worry I see there.

Once the four of us are lined up on the stage, Brock takes the podium and addresses the crowd. "Welcome, everyone. We are so pleased to announce that our latest foursome is back among us! Now that things have settled down, we are pleased to offer Sadie and the rest of her quad sanctuary once more." He stops, and the crowd claps and whoops loudly.

"Thank you, I'm excited as well. It has been hard, this transition in leadership. And it was never something I dreamed would happen, or wanted. However, I stand before you humbly willing to accept your vote, and become the new leader of the Resistance."

A chant begins at the back of the crowd, and slowly gains momentum "Ri-sing! Ri-sing! Ri-sing!" Before long, nothing else can be heard but the urgent call of the people. Finally, Brock raises both hands, and they fall silent.

He raises his voice, and at the top of his lungs he shouts, "The people are RISING!" The cheer in response is deafening.

He turns, grin in place, and fixes Patrick in his steely gaze. "Would you care to address the people? You've received such a warm welcome, I think they'd like to hear from you."

"Certainly!" Patrick enthuses and gives a quick wave to the crowd as he takes his place behind the podium.

"Hello everyone, thank you for the warm welcome. Truly, it means so much to have your support for our family. We are happy to be back among you, and we have news that we think you'll find joyous." He gives me a wink. "Sadie is pregnant! We've got a baby on the way."

Another deafening cheer goes up, and Patrick lets everyone go wild for a minute, before gesturing that he's got more to say.

"Thank you. We're over the moon, ourselves. Right, Sadie?" he asks and I nod happily. "However, we've got less than amazing news. It turns out, Helena wasn't the only person in leadership here who was a danger to our family."

A rumble of shock and dismay ripples through the crowd, but Patrick doesn't stop to let them process.

"In fact, there's an even bigger snake in our midst, and I, for one, think it's time the people knew the truth. Don't you, Brock?"

His eyes narrow dangerously. "What's this about, Royce?"

"Oh, you would know. The snake is you, Brock. Or, should I call you Brody? I'm not sure which is your real name. Either way, you're in hot water." At hearing his *other* name, panic crosses the older man's face. He motions to Ryker, the intelligence agent standing to his left, who reaches for a gun. But Atlas is faster, and grabs the man's arm before he even makes it to the holster. Disarming him with a flick of the wrist, Atlas dodges a punch, and slams a fist into the side of his face. Ryker crumples to the stage in a heap.

"Brock, that's unnecessary, really. Is that any way to treat your guests? We're just going to enlighten everyone here about what's going on. You see, Brock here has been leading quite the double life. Turns out, Helena wasn't his only paramour. No, unfortunately, my mother was also one of them. Some of you may know her as the queen of the NAA."

The silence is so profound, you can hear the wind rustle the leaves on the trees.

"I don't know how many others there are, I only know that we have traced lead after lead, and everything points back to you, Brock. The trust—the one which demanded construction of the Environmental Impact Centers, where hundreds of women were kept drugged and pregnant—is currently controlled by Branson Richardson. Satellite Security belongs to one Brody Richardson, who seduced my mother and convinced her to help him over-throw the government of the NAA. Oh! And he's the supposed *cousin* of Branson Richardson. And Brock here, plotting and taking over the Resistance by slowly poisoning Helena's mind over the years to gain leadership. Did any of you know his last name was Richardson? No, me either." He looks around for a moment, and then snaps. "Oh, yeah. Here are the photo IDs on file with the NAA for each of those three cousins! You've been a busy, busy man over the years, Brock." He points to the large projection screen across the way, which flickers one, and then shows three IDs side by side. Each one has the name of a different Richardson, but a photo of Brock, with various ages and hair styles represented.

"Did I leave anything out?" He looks at me, and I shake my head no.

"All right, then. Brock Richardson, you're hereby under arrest for crimes against humanity, including but not limited to kidnapping, medical slavery of more than four hundred women, as well as stealing thousands of the resulting infants from their mothers."

I'm horrified as Brock leaps across the stage at Patrick, the knife in his hand flashing dull black as he flies through the air. Patrick doesn't miss a beat, and dodges to the side, knocking the swipe wide. Brock pulls up mid stride, and turns to swing at Patrick's exposed side, but the strike doesn't land. The crowd surges forward, and two furious men grab hold of his ankle from the edge of the stage, and snatch. A moment of panic crosses his face before he's swallowed up by the raging mob.

Retreating to the back of the podium, Atlas shoves me behind him, next to Nell. Patrick makes his way over.

"Have you called for pickup?" he asks, but rather than answer, Atlas points. We all look, and there's Mav's jumbo helicopter, making great time over the tree line. The crowd quiets as she comes in to land, and they're buffeted by the wind from the double rotors. She sets it down directly behind the podium, and climbs out. The last few rotations blow her short curls as she hauls herself up the back side of the podium with a hand from Patrick.

She purses her lips with anger when she sees the angry crowd, and strides to the abandoned podium. "Now y'all better listen up, and listen *good.*" The crowd begins to look in her direction, but not fast enough to suit her. She pulls a double-barreled pistol from a holster I didn't know she had, and fires three rapid shots into the air. Everyone ducks and freezes, exactly the intended result.

I spot a bruised and battered—but still breathing—Brock, slung between a couple of men towards the back of the group.

"Y'all are behaving like a bunch of ill-mannered hooligans! Is this what you want to go down as the end of the Resistance? Because I sure as hell don't. Now, y'all hand that man over so he can be tried in a court of law. Settle yourselves, and figure out who gone' clean up this mess he done made. If y'all want a *chance* to govern yourselves, you best act like you got common sense." She gives them all a stare down that would make Mama Taylor proud, before turning and nodding to the four of us, clustered at the back of the stage.

We watch as Brock is reluctantly delivered to the stage, where Atlas cuffs him, and loads him into Mav's helicopter for transport. Groups begin to break up, as factions already start posturing for who should be the next leader. Looking over my shoulder, fully half of the prior leadership have vanished, while the rest are dispersed in the crowd campaigning to take on the vacated role.

We are about to board the helicopter ourselves when a shout draws our attention.

"Wait, all of you!" The petite spitfire who used to be our neighbor jogs over, hair wild in the chopper's down-draft.

"Halle!" I shout back in surprise, before crossing to give her a hug, Nell hot on my heels. The three of us exchange a quick embrace, and then stay huddled close to hear her over the noise.

"What's going to happen to the Resistance? If Patrick is here to arrest Brock, the NAA knows about us, and our location. Do we need to evacuate?" She levels me with a frank stare, and I look back over my shoulder at Patrick, where he's strapping himself into the chopper.

"No, elect a fair leader, and give us a call. We want *all* of our citizens to be free."

Relief floods her features, and I feel her shoulders sag beneath my arm. "Thank you, Sadie. I'll make sure it happens." With one final squeeze, she jogs back out from under the blades, and we board the chopper.

"What did she want?" Patrick yells.

"To know if we were going to wipe them out."

He shakes his head sadly. "I hate that they're afraid of that. Hopefully they'll figure it out, and we never have to step in."

I don't respond, instead looking out the window as we slowly hover away from the earth, gaining altitude quickly. Our last view before making the final turn and flying away is of Halle behind the podium, giving orders. *I think they'll be just fine.*

TWENTY-FIVE

EPILOGUE—
UNRAVELED

I t took months to undo the evil that was perpetrated under Patrick's father's nose. We were able to wake and find family or provide homes for ninety percent of the women who were formerly captive. Brock is behind bars, serving a life sentence. The remaining ten percent are receiving the best care our scientists can provide them, and moved to the medical facilities closest to their families. Children are being reunited with biological mothers they didn't get a chance to know, and all of the births in the last five months have been to mothers who were awake, and of sound mind. The further we dug, the more corruption we found and had to root out. Frankly, I'm not sure it's all gone yet, but I know we'll never stop searching, and never stop fighting for the freedom of our people. I let out a tired groan as a large white medical hov-truck slowly makes its way down the hospital drive, loaded with the last six women being returned to their hometowns.

"Well, that's the last woman, finally going home," Patrick says, voice tired but with a note of satisfaction.

I don't share his sense of a job well done. "Yes, but so many of them are just being moved to new facilities until we figure out how to wake them. It feels like failure, Patrick." The defeat and regret in my tone are clear, even to my own ears. I cautiously lower myself down onto the concrete step at the back of the hospital. My belly is huge and moving anywhere takes some time.

Patrick drops down next to me, and slips his arm around my shoulders, pulling me gently to his side. He plants a kiss on the top of my head, and I can't help but smile. *Some things never change.*

"That's no way to look at it, Sadie. It's not perfect, but I'm still calling what we've accomplished a win. We aren't going to give up until every last woman is awake, or her family is ready to let go." His other hand comes around, and gently lifts my chin, so I'm eye to eye with him. "I promise."

I give him a quick peck on the lips. "I know, we're doing everything we can. And you're right, it is great. It's . . . overwhelming." Messages from the other women, the families, even the older children grateful to be reunited with their loved ones are pouring in daily. My mind replays our tearful reunion with Josephine, and how great it felt to wrap her in a huge bear hug and have her hug us right back. She was angry about what had been done to her, but she was awake to be angry, and she would take the time she needed to process. They all would.

"It is, but we're not alone. The doctors are doing their best, and I got word from Zanetti this morning, that their scientists have a moss that grows there that they use as an anti-paralytic that they think could lead to something useful."

Hope blossoms in my heart, but another problem rears its ugly head. "That's amazing, but we still have to deal with the cabals getting bolder and trying to snatch women in broad daylight . . ."

"Atlas and Nell are on it, Sadie. They won't stop hunting until the cabals are dealt with, one way or another." His voice is full of confidence.

It would have to do, for now. "So, what now?" I ask, staring out at the setting sun on the pine trees.

He hums happily. "Now, we go home."

I groan. "Patrick, the shoebox of an apartment we're staying in here is *not* home. Don't insult the word home by applying it to that sad, tan place. But yes, we can go back *to the apartment*," I agree tiredly, and push to my feet.

"I agree, which is why we're not going back to the apartment tonight. We're all packed. We're going *home*."

My jaw drops in surprise. "Home, like . . . where? Where do we even live now, Patrick, if we're not going from tri-state to tri-state, overseeing the wake ups and helping the women transition back to normal life?"

"I guess you'll have to wait and see." He crooks a finger at me, a mischievous grin plastered on his handsome face. We climb into our NAA-issued hov-car, and Patrick gives the driver a nod. Not a word passes between them, but he pulls out of the hospital drive, and takes the first interstate due south.

We're going home.

TWENTY-SIX

BONUS EPILOGUE

Some time later

Patrick's face appears on my comm device, startling me from my thoughts, and the tray of brownies I was about to put into the oven. "Oh, hey, hon. How are things going there?"

He smiles. "Good, just calling to give you a report from today's meetings." He runs a hand through his hair, which is long enough to brush the collar of his shirt. He grows it longer now, and it suits him. The first hints of gray have started to add some salt to his dark locks, and he looks even better than the day we first met. The crown is a heavy responsibility, but he wears it well since his father stepped down a few years ago.

"Great, lay it on me."

"Well, construction on the last train station in the Alaska Territories is on schedule to be completed next month, so the NLC there will be open for business within four to six months, right on time."

"Always good to hear."

"Yes, my thoughts exactly. The new expansions on the Bachelor Book have gone over like gangbusters, and our match rate is through the roof with Glitch at the helm. The tri-states with fully operational electric trains since last year are seeing thirty percent growth on matches, and have a fifteen percent higher birth rate than the old system, already."

At that, I can't suppress my grin. "So, we held steady this year?" I prod for the number that's most important.

"I'm proud to announce that our population *grew* one percent over last year's numbers."

I clap, thrilled to hear that the modifications we've put into place were having a positive effect for our people. After the corruption was uncovered, the people were ready for change. We implemented quite a few initiatives, but the most important were all overhauls to the NLC and compulsory marriage program. For starters, it's no longer compulsory. And the data has been provided to the people in the matching program so that each and every individual can see their stats, and potential fertility ratings with anyone in the Bachelor Book. We decided to keep the name, and there was now an accompanying Bachelorette Book, for the guys—that was Glitch's idea.

To facilitate more successful matches, the NLCs are all open and operational, on a "schedule your own time" basis. Any couple that wants to meet can take the nearest NAA train to a predetermined NLC, and spend as much or as little time together as they'd like. If they hit it off, they can be married, and receive any fertility assistance they require in house, no matter their fertility rating. If needed, egg and sperm donations are available to help them conceive when they're ready. So far, the public has received the changes incredibly well.

"That's exactly why your popularity ratings are through the roof, my love," I say in a sing-song voice.

"That's why *our* popularity ratings are through the roof," he corrects me.

"Fine, ours. When are you heading home?" I ask, propping my hip on the oven handle.

"Mav says we can leave in about an hour. I'll be in late, though. So don't wait up. You need your rest." He gives me his best stern tone, but he knows I'll be up waiting for him, just like I am any time he's called away to the capitol without me.

"Sure, dear." I wink.

"Impossible woman—it's a good thing I'm in love with you."

"Yes, it is. See you soon."

A kick to my spleen wakes me with a start. With a groan, I roll to my side, placing a hand on my swollen belly. "Okay, okay, I'm getting up. Your temper is going to drive me crazy, isn't it, PJ?" I rub my hand affectionately over the bump, anticipating my little one's arrival any time in the next few weeks. As I climb to my feet, happy screeches filter through our closed bedroom door, and I smile. The sound of running feet coalesce at my doorway, and Patrick's voice calls them back from the other room. *Bless him for trying to let me get some sleep.*

After taking care of my morning routine, I walk barefooted out of our bedroom, the burnished pine floors smooth underfoot. My brothers poured a lot of love into this home for us. Sun filters through the windows that line the entire back of the house floor to ceiling, overlooking the pasture where Morgan grazes, although currently he's lazing at the fence line, nosing around for treats dropped from small fingers. I enter the kitchen and find a cup of cocoa, warm and waiting for me. Grabbing it with grateful fingers, I take small sips as I make my way out and onto the back porch.

Hovering in the doorway, I see all of my loves in one room. Patrick is giving Penelope a piggy-back ride around the perimeter of the porch. Her short black pig-tails bounce as he runs, and her giggles hang in the air like magic. Growing tired of the game, she demands to be put down, and he obliges. You don't argue with a two-year-old, even if you are king of the NAA.

Jacqueline, our oldest girl sits across a checkerboard from our son and middle child, Zane. "That's just not how it works, Zane. You can't skip two without touching a space in between."

Zane pouts, sticking his lip far enough out to land an airplane on. "I don't like this game."

Jacqueline, already diplomatic for her age, bargains with him. "Finish this round and you can choose the next two games."

He perks up and moves the offending piece back where it was before. I smile, and Patrick catches my gaze from across the way. He walks over, and plants a lingering kiss on my lips. His hands on my hips hold me close, and then navigate around to my belly as he bends down to speak to our newest addition.

"PJ, are you ready to come out yet? Mama's hogging you," he whispers conspiratorially.

I snort in response. "It's not *hogging* him, I'm *growing* him." We *have had this argument the last month of every pregnancy.*

"I know, I'm extra excited, since you finally let me name one after myself." He grins ear to ear while continuing to rub my belly, and I groan.

"I'm regretting that decision. Maybe we'll name him Paul. Pierre? Percy!" I tease, and he waggles his eyebrows at me.

"Nice try, Queen Sadie. But I'm not falling for that one. You're far too honest. This baby is Patrick Junior." He smacks another happy kiss on my cheek.

Queen Sadie. That took a long time to get used to, but in the end, it was my decision to accept it. Patrick was made to rule, and there's no one I trust more to ensure our family's safety than ourselves. So, we assumed the role when his father stepped down after Jacqueline's first birthday. It wasn't as much time as we'd planned, but he was ready to leave the spotlight after "The Deb Debacle" was in headlines daily for months. Patrick's mother was still serving her treason sentence on house arrest, in a separate estate from his father's current residence. It pained him, but they were adults. They had to work out their issues—or not—as they saw fit.

The kids spot us and run over, nearly taking me out from the waist down with their enthusiasm. "Mama, Mama! Up, up!" Penelope clenches her hands at me in anticipation, and I lean down to pick her up, and then settle her on my hip. Patrick takes my now-empty cocoa mug so I have two hands free to snuggle her. Jacqueline and Zane are right back to their checkers game, after the brief greeting. *They grow up way too fast.*

A knock on the front door interrupts our quiet moment, and Patrick pats me on the shoulder as he walks by. "I'll get it. Your mom's bringing the food for family lunch."

"Jacqueline, Zane! Granny and Papa are here with lunch! Why don't you go help them carry it?" I urge, and they skitter past me.

I hear Mav call out from somewhere behind me in the house, "Where are those delicious children! Nom, nom, nom!"

Squeals—of delight, and terror—ensue as they run from her scariest troll voice. "Mimi, stop! Did you bring us anything?"

She sighs. "Of course, you rotten things. Come see Mimi for your gifts."

I shake my head at their antics, but don't interfere as I walk past them to the dining room. She loves bringing them treasures from all over the globe, in her role as Captain of the NAA Airforce. I'm pretty sure that's why she volunteers to bring Patrick home every month from the capitol. When the kids are older, we'll all go with him on his monthly journeys, but for now, we want them to grow up slowly, and out of the spotlight.

"Your parents are here, all the brothers and nieces and nephews," Patrick murmurs as I join him in the doorway, and he takes Penelope off my hip. "It's a full house today."

I give him a warm smile before responding, "Just how we like it."

"Just how we like it," he agrees.

Hey, Readers! Thank you so much for coming along on this journey with me! For quite a while, this was the last book planned for the Populations Crumble world. Frankly, I was too happy with how it ended to consider messing it up by writing more. But . . . you asked. Reader after reader left comments, asking for more in this world. And one day, it hit me. There *is* another story to tell.

Y'all. I'm excited, and I hope you are too.

Dive straight into Marked now!

What readers are saying:

"I loved this world. Okay, there are parts of it that aren't so good, but on the whole, I was taken with Demy and saw what she

215

saw. There is lots of action and it's also very emotional. The choice Demy has to make is incredibly tough. I know which way I'd go, as it stands right now, but Im hedging my bets because I have no idea which way this story is going to go. And I love that! " – Merissa, The Archeolibrarian on Goodreads

"I was freaking excited when I read the blurb for this one. It was filled with great characters/friendships, captivating writing and a fast-paced plot. I was rooted to the story and hanging on to every word. I loved how the author introduced the 3 potential love inter-ests (although I know who I want her to end up with) it was nice to see their different characterizations! Now let's talk about our main character Demy. She was an easy character to love especially considering how her story started. She was constantly on the run so the intensity and action-packed of the story definitely raised the stakes. " – Goodreads Reviewer

TWENTY-SEVEN
EASTER EGGS

Hey Readers, thank you so much for spending your time with me on this journey with Patrick and Sadie through the Populations Crumble trilogy. They had quite a few ups and downs, and so did I, as this is the first series I've ever written and published. I thought you might enjoy a few tidbits about the stories, and a peek behind the curtain, if you will.

Jackson Flats is loosely based on the actual geographic location of Jacksonville, Florida. The area descriptions are fairly accurate to the more rural areas, and the pines and palms are native Florida flora.

My dad was a horseman growing up, in a poor family where you grew most of your own food, and worked hard every day to make a better life. He had a permanent scar on one lip where his childhood pony ran him under his mother's clothes line, and snatched him from his back. Eventually, he grew up and married and moved on, but the horse bug bit me early in life. I grew up listening to his stories of horsemanship, and one of his favorite books that I in turn read was Justin Morgan Had a Horse by Marguerite Henry. After years of pleading, my parents finally succumbed and bought me my very own horse, a beautiful bay mare named Desi. For Sadie's best horse friend, there was no other name I could choose but **Morgan**. The scenes involving horses were all based on my own experience of nearly ten years of horsemanship.

The house number **1712** assigned to Sadie and the crew in the Resistance compound is the same number as the townhouse Dustin and I bought as newlyweds.

Zanetti is a real mountain, located in the Wrangell-St. Elias National Park and Preserve in Alaska, USA. My husband and I visited Alaska in 2016, and the place is a beautiful blend of native and western cultures. We were particularly awed in our wanderings by the beautiful creations and rich history of the Tlingit people, which is where I drew a spark of inspiration. However, the People of Zanetti and their home under the mountain are a work of my imagination, and not representative of any particular group's customs or lore.

There are many other small tidbits and pieces of me tucked into the story, but I'll leave the rest to your own imagination. If you've loved the journey so far, your review would mean the world to me. As a new author, I read every single one and cherish your kind words.

Love and Books,

K. A. Gandy

ABOUT THE AUTHOR

K. A. Gandy was born and raised in Jacksonville, Florida, and is married with two kids. She has worked as a restaurant hostess, library book shelver, ranch hand, tour guide, Realtor, tech whiz, landlord, and small business consultant, all in addition to pursuing her passion for writing. As a person of many interests, her life has never been boring. She likes to write late in the evenings and thinks drinking hot tea and baking great cookies fuels hopes and dreams. If you would like to find more of her works, you can sign up for her newsletter at https://www.subscribepage.com/e0v1b 5. You can also get updates on Facebook at https://www.facebo ok.com/KAGandyAuthor.

MORE BY K. A. GANDY

Post-Apoc

In The Dust

Finding the Bastion

Descendants of Rust – Pre-order Now!

Dystopian

Dwindle (Populations Crumble, Book 1)
Torn from her home and family. Forced to marry a genetically matched stranger. Will she find love, or destruction?

Rise (Populations Crumble, Book 2)
The man she thought she knew truly is a stranger. Swept away on their honeymoon, the stakes have never been higher. Will his identity be their undoing, or will they rise together?

Reign (Populations Crumble, Book 3)
Kidnapped from their honeymoon resort, nothing is as it seems. Betrayal, intrigue, and secrets abound as Sadie works to free the captive women. But will she end up the savior, or the next captive?

Marked(Populations Crumble: Resurgence, Book 1)
She doesn't want to get married, but with her would-be captors on her heels, she's got no choice but to hope the NLC's strict security protocols will be a safe haven. Marriage is a small price to pay for her life, after all.

Fantasy

Aerthen Sight (An'Loran Chronicles, FREE Prequel Short)

The Lost Talisman(An'Loran Chronicles, Book 1)

The Hatchling – Pre-order now!(An'Loran Chronicles, Book 2)

Clean & Small-Town Romance (as Kristen Dixon)

Bea Mine (Sweet Nothings Bake Shop, Book 1)

Will Travel for Love (Sweet Nothings Bake Shop, Book 2)

Waiting on Forever (Sweet Nothings Bake Shop, Book 3)

The Bachelor Bargain (Sweet Nothings Bake Shop, Book 4)

Sweet Romance Anthology (Paperback Only)

www.ingramcontent.com/pod-product-compliance
Lightning Source LLC
Chambersburg PA
CBHW022007050726
47499CB00003BA/714